HIDE AND SEEK

LANTERN BEACH GUARDIANS, BOOK 1

CHRISTY BARRITT

CHAPTER ONE

THE WEATHER—AND God—had created the windswept barrier island Cassidy Chambers called home. Both were forces to be reckoned with, and the storm that raged around her reminded her of that fact.

Lightning flashed across the dark sky like an electrical circuit on display, and thunder clapped in twisted applause of the show. The wind gusted through the porch screens around her, causing Cassidy's hair to rise in what felt like supernatural swirls, almost as if it had taken on a mind of its own.

Normally, Cassidy might enjoy the storm. But tonight nothing felt right.

Nothing.

She wasn't sure when her world would feel normal again.

As Cassidy stared at the dark ocean just across the dune, the door opened behind her. A moment later, her husband wrapped his arms around her waist before nuzzling her neck, his warm lips brushing her delicate skin.

"What's wrong?" Ty murmured, still holding her.

"I don't know." Cassidy frowned, not taking her eyes from the beach or the storm. "I have a bad feeling in my gut."

As she said the words, another strong wind swept around her. Forecasters had warned the storm would be a doozy. Cassidy and Ty had spent a good portion of the afternoon securing items outside their house so gusts wouldn't carry anything away.

"You've got good instincts," Ty said, his head still nestled next to hers. "Do you think this is about the storm?"

Cassidy's jaws clenched at his question. She'd been sitting on the couch, trying to unwind by reading a new suspense novel she'd gotten in the mail, when the feeling hit her. She hadn't been able to ignore it.

"I wish I knew," she said. "But I don't. Something's just bothering me."

Rain sprayed the side of the house, sounding almost like a barrage of bullets.

Ty took her hand and tugged her toward the door. “I started a fire inside. Why don’t you come in and get warm?”

A fire with Ty at her side sounded nice—more than nice. It sounded perfect.

But Cassidy couldn’t leave yet. Not until some tension left her chest.

“Just a few more minutes,” she said. “Then I’ll go inside. I promise.”

Ty moved closer and stared at the horizon with her. Because of the weather and the darkness, it was nearly impossible to see anything. But occasionally the lightning gave them a glimpse of angry white-capped waves storming the sandy shores.

It was April, and the ocean water was still cold. In a couple of months, tourists would flock these shores. But, for now, the island community of Lantern Beach enjoyed a moment of serenity.

Tourists were great. They helped provide a livelihood for many on this island. But the moments of rest were also welcome. The island’s schedule almost mirrored the ebb and flow of the tide—crashing then receding only to repeat the process.

Cassidy was the police chief in town, and even

though the community was relatively small and quiet, she definitely had her hands full. In fact, this place, with its secluded, hard-to-reach location, had more than its fair share of crimes.

As lightning lit the sky again, her breath caught. She squinted as she stared at the shore in the distance, tension threading through her muscles. “Did you see that?”

Ty straightened. “See what?”

“It looked like something on the beach.”

“Probably some debris from the storm. You never know what you’ll find. Austin just found that old Harley Davidson motorcycle that washed up during a storm in the fall.”

Cassidy remembered hearing Austin’s story. But she sensed this was something far different.

Her instinct seemed to throb along with her pulse as she waited for answers, for confirmation.

She kept her eyes fastened on the sand in front of her. At any moment, more lightning should fill the sky. She needed that illumination to prove she’d seen something.

Until then, her lungs felt frozen with apprehension.

Ty nodded toward the screen door that led to a

wooden stairway that eventually led to the beach. "Do you want to go check it out?"

His words caused a rush of gratitude.

Ty was *such* a good husband—supportive, patient, and kind. He was everything Cassidy could have ever wanted and more than she ever deserved in a life partner.

She was nearly certain Ty felt the same way about her, which pretty much made them the perfect match.

Cassidy thanked God every day for bringing him into her life.

She still waited for that lightning, unable to look away from the beach. "Let's wait and see if we can get another glimpse."

Walking on the beach on an evening like this would be no easy task. According to forecasters, wind gusts could be up to fifty miles an hour. The rain would feel like lead pellets bombarding her skin.

Cassidy stared out at the water and held her breath, waiting to see if her eyes had deceived her. Part of her hoped she had been seeing things. That her gut was wrong.

Finally, electricity branched across the sky.

As the horizon lit, Cassidy spotted something out of place on the shoreline.

Something had definitely washed up in the storm.

She couldn't be sure, but it almost looked like a life jacket.

With someone still strapped inside.

"Is that . . . ?" Ty muttered.

Cassidy took off toward the door, knowing they had no time to waste.

They needed to get out there and see what was going on.

Now.

CASSIDY'S FEET dug into the sand as she raced over the dune. The wind gusted again, almost as if urging her to stay inside.

But she couldn't do that.

Ty and Kujo surged ahead. The former Navy SEAL always had a leg up on her physically. She was grateful for his strength now. She needed it.

As they crested the dune, another bolt of lightning lit the way for them.

Cassidy spotted the life jacket again.

This time, she confirmed that arms and legs protruded from it.

Someone had definitely washed up on the shore.

As Kujo barked at the figure, Ty fell onto his knees beside their victim. When Cassidy saw the look on his face, her breath caught.

Something was wrong. Really wrong.

She dropped to the ground beside Ty.

She sucked in a breath as concern slammed into her chest.

"She's just a child," Cassidy muttered.

A girl. Probably six or seven. Small. Innocent. Vulnerable.

Her eyes were closed, and her dark hair was plastered to her face.

"She has a pulse, but it's faint." Ty began CPR as Cassidy pulled the phone from her pocket and called the station. She and Ty were going to need all the help they could get to figure out what happened.

With backup on the way, Cassidy put away her phone and turned back to Ty. He continued to do chest compressions on the tiny, nearly lifeless figure.

Dear Lord, please be with this girl. Help her. Save her.

As a chill washed over Cassidy, she glanced up and down the shore.

She didn't see any other life jackets. Nothing else that concerned her as much as this child's life did.

As the wind swept around them and more rain pelted their skin, the girl twitched.

Then coughed.

Ty turned her to her side as water sputtered from her mouth.

Her eyes jerked open, and fear seemed to fill the air around her.

"It's going to be okay." In one motion, Ty scooped the girl into his arms.

They had to get this child out of the elements. Had to get her warm. The next few minutes would be critical.

With Kujo at their heels, they hurried to their cottage.

Her officers would be here soon to check out the rest of the beach. Paramedics would also check out the girl.

But the bad feeling remained in Cassidy's gut.

She would worry about that later.

Right now, she wanted to focus all her attention on this girl—and make sure she was okay.

CHAPTER TWO

AS TY WRAPPED a blanket around the girl's shoulders, Cassidy kneeled in front of her. The girl sat on the couch—on the edge—with her eyes wide.

Cassidy had found some old clothing—a child-sized T-shirt and some leggings—in the trunk of her police SUV. She kept a few changes of clothing there, in all sizes, just in case others needed them during emergencies.

Kujo dutifully laid at the child's feet, instinctively seeming to know he needed to protect the girl.

As Cassidy studied the child, she didn't see signs of any hidden injuries. But she could only imagine the turmoil she might have gone through.

Cassidy offered a soft smile and kept her voice

gentle as she said, “My name is Cassidy, and I’m a police officer. Can you tell me your name?”

The girl only stared, her gaze almost hollow.

But she said nothing.

Cassidy waited, hoping the girl would find her voice. She desperately wanted to ask questions, to find some answers.

She needed to call the child’s parents. They must be so worried.

But it all started with a name. There hadn’t been any missing children’s reports in the area. Without any information from the girl, this would be a lot harder.

“You can’t share your name?” Cassidy continued.

The girl still didn’t say anything.

After another moment, Ty rose. “How about if I go fix some hot chocolate to warm you up? How does that sound?”

The girl stared.

Cassidy gave Ty a nod, hoping her gratitude showed through in her gaze. The drink could help warm the girl—and maybe she’d eventually open up.

Thank the Lord, she’d survived whatever ordeal she’d gone through.

She was safe now, but Cassidy had a feeling this

was just the beginning.

What kind of secrets lingered behind this girl's eyes?

She must be so scared to be here without her parents.

Her parents . . .

Cassidy held back a frown at the thought of them.

Where were they? Out on the water? Had an SOS been issued? Certainly she would have heard.

Her phone rang. She glanced at the screen and saw it was Officer Braden Dillinger.

As she rose to take the call, Ty traded places with her. He handed the girl a cup of hot chocolate then sat beside her.

Confident that the girl was in good hands, Cassidy stepped down the hallway and put the phone to her ear.

"Dillinger," she started. "What's going on?"

Wind hit the speaker, making it hard to understand anything Dillinger said. "Shipwreck" and "debris" was all Cassidy could make out.

Her back muscles tightened.

"Have you found any more victims?" she asked.

More static sounded on the line until finally Cassidy heard a "no."

She wasn't sure if the answer made her feel relieved or tenser.

She wanted to be out there investigating for herself. But, when she looked into the girl's wide eyes, she knew she couldn't do that. Cassidy couldn't leave the child in her time of distress. She needed to trust her officers right now.

"Let me know if you hear or see anything else," Cassidy said.

"Roger that."

She slipped the phone into her pocket and walked back into the living room. She stepped closer just in time to see Ty doing the disappearing coin trick for the girl. When the dime appeared behind the child's ear, a small smile tugged at her lips.

Cassidy paused to absorb the moment.

Ty would be *such* a good dad. He'd always had a way with kids.

Something about that thought made her heart sag.

She wasn't sure that would ever be a reality.

She turned from those thoughts and glanced at the girl again.

Maybe Cassidy didn't need to stay inside after all. Ty had a handle on the situation. Besides, their Jane Doe didn't seem ready to talk.

Or was it more than that?

Was the girl unable to speak?

Concern surged in Cassidy.

Only time would tell.

Cassidy pointed toward the beach, indicating to Ty that she needed to attend to something. He nodded to let her know it was okay.

She pulled on a rain slicker she kept on a hanger near the door.

As she stepped onto her screened porch, the life jacket they'd taken off the girl caught her eye.

Cassidy pulled out her phone and snapped a few pictures. Maybe something on the life jacket would indicate where the girl had come from.

She examined it a moment. The vest appeared to be a generic brand with no clues.

Had the girl been on a boating expedition with her parents when the storm caught them by surprise?

Or maybe she'd come from a cruise ship. Crews from the vessels had to call for Coast Guard assistance at times as they made their way down the coast. Had this little girl somehow fallen overboard? Or jumped?

But if she'd fallen over, she wouldn't have a life jacket.

As the questions churned in Cassidy's head, she made quick phone calls to the Coast Guard and the marine police.

No maydays had been reported.

She turned the life jacket over and looked at the bottom edge.

As she did, she squinted.

Something had been written there in black marker, something she hadn't been able to see in the darkness.

Cassidy held it closer, trying to make out the letters.

She sucked in a breath as the words came into focus.

Cassidy Chambers.

Her name had been written on the child-size life jacket.

What sense did that make?

The bad feeling in Cassidy's gut turned into something much bigger and much more ferocious at the sight.

CASSIDY TUCKED the life jacket inside her house for safekeeping before hurrying toward the beach.

Two of her officers were there investigating.

She wondered if anything else had washed up.

Just as before, the wind pushed at her, urging her to stay away. Rain hit her slicker in frigid drops that almost took her breath away. Thunder and lightning danced in the sky around her, almost as if warning her that things were just getting started.

She crested the dune again.

As the sky lit, she spotted her officers with flashlights bobbing farther down the shore. It looked like a few other objects had washed up, but Cassidy couldn't get a good look at them.

Instead of investigating the items, she strode toward Dillinger. "Anything?"

He nodded toward one of the objects. "We've found a cooler, a trash bag, and a piece of wood. Bradshaw headed farther down the beach to see if there's anything there. So far, he hasn't found anything."

Cassidy pressed her lips together. Not enough wreckage had washed ashore to indicate a ship had wrecked. She'd expect more broken boards and pieces of fiberglass if that was the case.

So what happened here?

She turned back to Dillinger, raising her voice to be heard over the storm. "I need you to photograph everything and then put them in your squad car. We're going to need to take anything we find back to the station and examine them for clues."

Dillinger squinted as water hit his face and flooded into his eyes. "What's going on, Chief?"

Cassidy turned away from the wind and frowned. "I don't know. That's what I need to figure out. But I found a girl washed up here on the beach. My name was written on her life jacket."

Dillinger's eyes widened. "You didn't recognize her?"

"Never seen her before, and she hasn't spoken a word since we rescued her."

"Weird."

"We need to make sure to search the area all around here. If this girl washed ashore, there's a good chance her parents or guardians are out here too. I already put in a call to the Coast Guard and marine police. They haven't had any emergency calls."

"We'll be thorough."

Before they could talk any more, Cassidy spotted flashing lights in the distance.

Paramedics were here.

Between all of them, hopefully they would find some answers.

CHAPTER THREE

DOC CLEMSON, the island physician, pulled Cassidy aside after his examination of the girl. The two of them stood in the kitchen, close enough to see their Jane Doe but far enough away for privacy.

Cassidy had asked him to come out. Though paramedics had done an initial assessment, Cassidy would feel better hearing Clemson's medical opinion.

"She appears to be in overall good health, all things considered." Doc Clemson pushed his wire-framed glasses up higher on his nose, his red hair disheveled from being awakened.

Cassidy stared across the room at the girl. She was dry now, and she sipped on her reheated hot chocolate. Ty had offered her some crackers, but she wasn't interested. Instead, she sat there with a vacant look in her eyes and a blanket around her shoulders.

Cassidy's heart thudded with a mixture of emotion—grief for the girl, gratitude they'd come upon her when they did, determination to find answers.

"There's no telling how long she was out there in the ocean," Cassidy said. "How did her little body even survive those conditions? The cold?"

She could only imagine the terror the girl had endured.

Clemson frowned. "Maybe she wasn't out there very long."

"We can hope." There was one more issue Cassidy needed to talk to him about, one that pressed hard on her right now. "She's not talking. Hasn't said a word since we found her. What's that about?"

Clemson pushed up his glasses again. "Sometimes mutism can occur after a traumatic experience. That would be my guess about what's going on here now."

That had been Cassidy's suspicion as well. "How long does it usually last?"

He let out a long breath as he glanced at the girl

again. "It's hard to say. Sometimes, it can be hours. Sometimes, days. Sometimes, much longer."

Cassidy crossed her arms over her chest, her gaze still lingering on the child. "I'll look to see if any new missing children's reports have come in, as well as run her prints through the system. But this whole thing is strange."

"I'll agree with that. I've lived on this island a long time, and I've never seen anything like this happen."

In her time as police chief, she'd never encountered a situation like this either. Her mind continued to race through what she needed to do. "I guess I need to put in a call to social services. They'll want to know about this."

"They will. I don't envy the tasks you have in front of you."

"I don't either." Cassidy snapped back into professional mode, realizing she'd allowed wistfulness to consume her voice. "Thank you so much for your help today."

Clemson grabbed his bag from the floor before tugging his coat tighter. "Anytime, Cassidy. Anytime."

With a nod at Ty, Doc started toward the door.

It didn't look like anyone was going to be getting any sleep anytime soon.

The storm wasn't letting up either. Wind still slammed into the house along with sheets of rain. Thankfully, the storm system wasn't supposed to bear down on them long—only a couple more hours before it would continue out to sea.

Before she got distracted, Cassidy got out her phone to call the county social services. This girl would need to be run through the system, and social services would want to document other details of this case.

Grief clutched Cassidy's chest at the thought. She wasn't sure why she felt so protective of the child, other than for obvious reasons. But the thought of her going to stay with someone else left Cassidy feeling unsettled.

Maybe it was because Cassidy's name was on that life jacket.

She still couldn't figure that one out.

With a sigh, she dialed the number for Gail Stevens, a social worker Cassidy had worked with before. Gail answered on the first ring, and Cassidy explained the situation.

"I'm not sure I can get there until morning," Gail

said. "Not with the storm and the ferries not running."

"We'll take good care of her until you can arrive," Cassidy said. "You have my word."

"In the meantime, I'll see if I can find out anything from local municipalities also."

"Thanks, Gail."

Cassidy ended the call. The thought of the girl staying here with her brought her a measure of comfort.

But she was a long way from being okay with this situation.

AN HOUR LATER, paramedics had cleared out. Cassidy's officers had been instructed to continue combing the beach, looking for any possible clues. And Jane Doe was sleeping on the couch with Kujo curled on the floor beside her.

Ty tucked a blanket over her then pulled Cassidy into the kitchen. She could tell he had something on his mind. Since officials had arrived on the scene, he'd remained in the background, focusing on the girl.

But now he obviously needed to say something.

Ty stepped close, worry in his gaze. "Your name was found on her life jacket?"

They hadn't had a chance to talk about this yet.

Cassidy nodded, still perplexed at that fact herself. "That's right. It doesn't make any sense."

Ty raised his eyebrows, tension stiffening his shoulders. "You've never seen her before, right?"

Cassidy glanced at the girl again. "I have a pretty good memory for faces. I don't ever remember seeing or meeting her."

He crossed one arm over his midsection and rubbed his jaw with his other hand. "This just keeps getting weirder and weirder. Why would your name be on that life jacket?"

Cassidy couldn't stop asking herself that question either. "I have no idea. Unless somebody *wanted* me to find her or for her to end up with me. But why?"

"Maybe someone thought she'd be safe with you."

"That's a possibility. I just feel so badly for her."

"We all do. The good news is, she appears okay."

"That *is* good news." Cassidy shook her head, knowing that this trauma ran much deeper than the physical. Still, it was a blessing the girl wasn't injured or in the hospital with hypothermia. "I have to figure out what happened to her, though."

"How are you going to do that?"

That was a great question. She would need to dig in and follow the evidence. She prayed it led her somewhere useful and not on a wild goose chase.

"A bag of trash washed up," Cassidy said. "I need to go back to the station and sift through everything inside. I also need to run this girl's photo and prints through our system, see if there's anything I can find out."

Ty nodded. "That sounds like a good place to start."

She studied the apprehension on his face. He didn't like this situation. But was that all there was to this? "Are you okay staying with her while I go to work?"

He let out a breath, his features softening slightly. "I should be fine. I'll call you if I need anything. But she probably just needs to sleep."

Cassidy stretched on her tiptoes and planted a quick kiss on his lips. "You're the best, Ty."

He leaned closer for a minute, as if absorbing her presence. Finally, he stepped back with a challenge in his gaze. "Find out who did this, Cassidy. If you need my help, let me know. My friends and I will do whatever's needed to make sure we find out some answers."

Ty helped to run an organization called Blackout. The security group was located here on the island and consisted of former Navy SEALs who'd been some of the best.

Sometimes, it was good to have connections—especially in times of crisis.

And that's exactly what this felt like.

CHAPTER FOUR

"WHAT DO YOU THINK THIS MEANS?" Officer Dillinger stared at the items from the trash bag that had been displayed on a table at the police station.

Cassidy had gathered her crew for a mandatory meeting.

Officer Dillinger was a former Special Forces officer who was married to Cassidy's best friend, Lisa.

Officer Dane Bradshaw and his dog, Ranger, had proven valuable on multiple occasions.

Officer Jonathan Banks came to the department just last year, a former highway patrol officer from South Dakota who'd decided to give up everything to live at the beach.

Paige Henderson manned the front desk. She'd

come in to monitor the phones in case anyone called in with a lead or missing person report.

Cassidy stared at the items that had washed ashore and shook her head. "That's a good question."

Most of what had been inside the small trash bag had amounted to nothing. A couple of potato chip wrappers. Several empty water bottles. A few used tissues.

And that was it.

The state lab might be able to grab some DNA from something or maybe even some fingerprints. But, most likely, the ocean water had destroyed any evidence.

The wooden board told them nothing—nothing that could be related to the girl they had found. It appeared to be a typical piece of lumber, the kind commonly used in construction. It could have been pulled out to sea by the tide and then spit out farther up the shore.

The cooler had been empty.

Basically, nothing they'd found had led them to any answers.

"Maybe the girl snuck out of a rental house and somehow stowed away on a boat," Dillinger said. "Maybe the storm whipped up and she toppled overboard. I can check the currents to see which way they're pushing things."

"If that's the case, why haven't her parents called us?"

"Maybe they haven't realized she's missing yet."

Cassidy frowned. "I suppose it's a possibility. But it doesn't explain why my name is on the life jacket."

Dillinger leaned back against the wall behind him. "True. Maybe someone put her in the water and wanted you to find her."

"There are a lot of holes in that theory," Cassidy said. "For one thing, how did they know I would find her?"

"Maybe they thought that even if someone else found her, when they saw your name, they'd seek you out."

"Maybe. But why? I don't know this girl."

Dillinger shrugged. "Maybe they've seen you here on the island. They could know you're the police chief. Maybe they're in trouble."

"It's a possibility. At this point, I guess anything is." No theories had risen to the surface. Maybe it was better that way. She needed to keep an open mind until the evidence—or the girl—started talking.

"This whole thing is just bizarre."

"You can say that again." Cassidy glanced at Banks. "Did you run her prints through the system?"

"I did." He stood at attention at the other end of the table. "No hits. It can take a while sometimes."

"Of course." Cassidy frowned but quickly concealed it. She wouldn't share her frustration with her officers—not yet at least.

"Did Doc say how long it might be until the girl starts speaking again?" Dillinger asked.

"He said it varies. There have been some cases where trauma-induced mutism never goes away. Let's hope that's not what happens here. Not just for the sake of the case, but for the sake of this little girl."

"What will happen to her if nobody steps forward to claim her?" Dillinger asked.

"She'll become a ward of the state, I suppose. She'll go into the foster care system." Even as Cassidy said the words, a bad feeling rumbled inside her. She didn't like the thought of that.

"Talk about trauma on top of trauma," Dillinger said.

"Tell me about it," Cassidy said. "We need to find answers so that doesn't happen."

"What's our next step?" Banks straightened, waiting for her direction.

"We're going to check everything that we've already checked. I want a team walking the beach to see if anything else has washed up, I want a fresh set of eyes on that computer search to see if any photos match her identity, and I'm going to personally re-examine all the evidence that we've found."

"Are you going to put out a press release?" Bradshaw asked. "See if anyone comes forward?"

Cassidy paused a moment before answering. "Not yet. If loving parents lost their child, they're going to come to us. Right now, until we know what happened to the girl, I don't want to put this information out to the public."

"Understood," Bradshaw said.

"That said, we don't have any time to waste," Cassidy continued. "I hope none of you were counting on getting any sleep tonight."

"We'll do whatever it takes to help this girl," Dillinger said. "I think I speak for all of us when I say that."

"That's what I like to hear," Cassidy said.

"We were taught by the best."

Dillinger offered a nod, letting her know he was talking about her.

Cassidy hoped that she didn't let him down.

TY CHAMBERS LET out a long breath and lowered himself into a slip-covered chair across from the couch.

He'd finally gotten Jane Doe back to sleep. The girl had awakened crying in terror. After a few minutes of uncontrollable sobbing, she didn't look any closer to settling down.

Ty had found an old teddy bear that someone had left at the house—probably his friend's daughter, Ada, if he had to guess—and gave it to her. She'd wrapped her arms around it and calmed enough to fall back asleep.

Ada sometimes lost track of the toys she brought over. And, in this case, Ty was grateful. He didn't know what he would've done otherwise.

Jane Doe still hadn't said a word since they found her. Traumatic mutism.

Just what had that girl been through?

His muscles tensed at the thought of it. Ty hoped no one had purposely hurt her. Because if they had . . .

He fisted his hands. If there was one thing people should never do, hurting a child was at the top of the list. Or the elderly. Or his wife.

Come to think of it, Ty had a long list of people he felt protective over.

Nothing would ever change that.

Cassidy had been right not to ignore her gut instinct earlier. Thank goodness she'd stayed strong. If that girl had been left on the beach much longer, hypothermia would have set in.

He leaned forward in his seat, his elbows against his legs and his hands clasped in front of him.

One thing still bothered him.

Why had Cassidy's name been found on that life jacket? It didn't make sense. And Ty wasn't sure it ever *would* make sense.

It couldn't be a coincidence. Someone had wanted Cassidy to find this girl.

Ty had lived in a world of terrorists and war for so long that he could sense trouble. He sensed it now.

Did this somehow tie in with his background? He didn't think so. But there were too many unknowns for him to be certain.

Hopefully, Cassidy would be able to quickly find answers.

Ty stood and paced toward the window. The lights in the house were off except for a single lamp in the corner.

It was the middle of the night, and law enforcement had cleared out an hour ago. Ty hadn't heard from Cassidy since she left, but he assumed she was at the police station doing her thing. She was very good at doing her thing.

This island was lucky to have her. Ty didn't say that just because he was her husband. He'd yet to find anybody on the island—at least anybody on the up and up—who would disagree with him.

He shoved the curtain aside and peered out into the darkness. The storm still raged outside. The rain wasn't as much of a concern as the wind and tides.

Had anything else washed up? Pieces of a shipwreck?

That still seemed like the most likely scenario.

Ty squinted as something caught his eye in the distance.

Was that a flashlight beam bobbing on the shore?

Was someone still out there?

He thought the last police car had left about an hour ago. One of the officers could have parked somewhere else, he supposed.

But something about the light bothered him.

Ty grabbed his phone and dialed Cassidy's

number. He halfway expected her to sound tired or discouraged when she answered. But she didn't.

She sounded ready to fight.

Atta girl.

Ty's gaze followed the light as it moved farther down the shoreline, coming in and out of his line of sight. "Listen, do you have any of your guys out here looking for clues on the beach?"

"No, they're all back here at the station now. Why?"

Ty narrowed his eyes. "Somebody's on the beach."

"What?" Her voice caught. "Why would somebody else be out there at this time of night?"

"That's what I'd like to know also."

"I'll send one of my guys out," Cassidy said.

"By the time they get here, this person's likely to be long gone. I'll see if Colton will go." Colton helped head up Blackout. The headquarters was only ten minutes down the street.

"If you don't mind, that would be great. Tell him to be careful. We don't know what's going on here."

No, they didn't.

And that's what made this situation even more dangerous.

CHAPTER FIVE

CASSIDY CONTINUED to stare at the evidence on the table, hoping that something she hadn't noticed before would pop out at her. So far, nothing.

She straightened as another gust of wind hit the building, throwing debris into the windows.

What a terrible night for such a storm. Sometimes she feared a hurricane would someday completely wipe out this island.

Ty had just called again. Colton had checked out the beach, but whoever had been out there was gone.

Why would somebody be out in this weather? Cassidy could understand if it was one of her guys. But the average person wouldn't just happen to be wandering the beach on a night like tonight.

Unless they were looking for something or . . . someone.

More unrest rumbled inside her.

A knock sounded at the door to the conference room.

She looked up and spotted Dillinger.

"Come in," she told him.

"Chief, I know this is a bad time because we're thinking about this girl that we found," he started. "But I just wanted to remind you that the governor is coming to Lantern Beach today to start his vacation. I got another email from his head of security. They want to make sure that every precaution is in place."

Cassidy rubbed her temples. That was right. With everything going on, she'd nearly forgotten.

She glanced at her watch.

They had six hours until he arrived.

He wanted privacy for his visit, and Cassidy couldn't blame him. Even political figures deserved a break from the limelight.

Cassidy had already gone through all the protocols for his arrival yesterday, and she felt confident his visit would be a success. Besides, he was bringing an entourage of people with him to help with his everyday tasks. All Governor Hollick would need to concentrate on was relaxing and enjoying himself.

She turned back to Dillinger. "Email the head of security and let him know that everything is in place and that the Lantern Beach PD is at their disposal if they need us."

"Will do."

Cassidy glanced down at the evidence one more time. She could stare at this all night, but answers wouldn't magically appear.

For now, the best thing she could do was to step away. In an hour, the sun would come up. As much as Cassidy would like to grab a quick nap, she knew that wouldn't be happening. Not right now.

But, in a little while, she did want to swing by her cottage to see how that little girl was doing.

Because things were only going to get busier from here.

And probably more complicated.

TY BRIGHTENED AS SOON as Cassidy stepped into the house.

The storm outside had finally moved offshore, and the sun was coming up. He'd glanced out the window earlier and had been happy to see the flooding had subsided. It appeared cleanup would be minimal—and that was a blessing.

As was the sunshine.

He started across the room and gave Cassidy a quick kiss on the cheek, wishing he could do more to ease her burdens. But, as police chief, there were some jobs only she could do.

Looking at her, he could tell everything was catching up with her. Circles lined the skin under her eyes, and her normally neat hair escaped from the bun she'd pulled behind her head. She still looked as beautiful as ever.

But Ty feared things were beginning to take a toll on her.

He affectionately rubbed her arms. "I wasn't expecting to see you so soon."

Her gaze traveled behind him. "How's everything going?"

He looked toward Jane Doe sitting on the couch hugging that teddy bear and watching a cartoon on TV while Kujo laid at her feet. "She woke up screaming and crying about an hour ago. She was obviously having a nightmare of some sort."

A frown tugged at Cassidy's lips. "Has she said anything yet?"

Ty shook his head. "Not yet. I was hoping she might open up, but that hasn't happened."

Disappointment stained her gaze until her eyes flickered back to him. "Thanks for staying with her last night."

"It was no problem. She wasn't any trouble." Ty paused and studied Cassidy's face for another minute.

Things hadn't felt totally normal between the two of them lately, not since that doctor's visit. Until the results came in, he had a feeling Cassidy would remain preoccupied and maybe even distant.

He cleared his throat, knowing this wasn't the time to bring matters like that up. "Is Social Services still coming today?"

"That's the plan." Cassidy glanced at her watch. "If Gail's able to catch the first ferry, that would put her arriving in a couple of hours."

"I see. When she gets here will she just . . . take her?" Something about the scenario made him feel uncomfortable, though he didn't know why.

"They'll find a foster family for her to stay with."

Ty's gaze probed into Cassidy's. "Do you think that's a good idea? What if she's in danger? If she needs protection?"

Cassidy hesitated, and trepidation stretched

through her gaze. "I don't know. I was hoping we would have more answers before the social worker arrived. I'm working as hard as I can but . . . so far we have nothing—nothing to prove she needs protection or that she's a runaway."

He resisted the urge to pull her into his arms. There would be time for that later. "I know you're working hard. Maybe I can buy some time if we need it. The last thing I want is to let Jane Doe leave here if it's to her detriment."

Cassidy's gaze flickered up to meet his. "What are you proposing?"

"I don't have any firm plans yet. But I can come up with something if needed.

"Let's wait and see what happens," Cassidy said. "For now, I'd like to talk to her for a minute."

"Of course."

Ty watched as Cassidy rolled her shoulders back and plastered on a smile before walking toward the girl. She practically transformed into another person. Not in a fake way. But Cassidy had to wear a lot of hats. Right now, she needed to tap into her nurturing side.

"Good morning." Cassidy knelt in front of their guest. "Do you remember me? I'm Cassidy. It looks like you got a bit of sleep."

The girl stared at Cassidy, her eyes still wide. But she said nothing.

"Have you had anything to eat?" Cassidy asked.

The girl stared.

Ty watched, wondering if the girl would respond in any way. So far, the child hadn't responded to him with even a nod or a headshake.

"The other day when I went to the store, I bought some Lucky Charms," Cassidy whispered, almost as if sharing a secret. "That cereal was my favorite when I was a little girl, but my mom hardly ever let me eat it. She said it had too much sugar. But every once in a while, I still like to have some anyway. Have you ever had them before?"

Ty held his breath, waiting to see if the girl would respond. The child's attention was clearly focused on Cassidy. Maybe Cassidy could somehow reach her.

But instead the girl just stared.

"How about if I get you some?" Cassidy said. "You should probably eat something."

Even though the child didn't respond, Cassidy went into the kitchen and poured some into a bowl. She didn't add any milk before carrying the cereal back to the girl.

The girl stared at the bowl before finally picking

up a colored marshmallow and placing it in her mouth.

Good. Cassidy was right. The girl did need to eat something.

Cassidy always had a way with people. It was just one more thing to love about her. He would give her everything in the world if he could.

But there were some things he had no control over.

His heart ached at the thought.

Cassidy started to say something else when her phone rang. She excused herself and stepped back toward Ty in the kitchen.

She put the cell on speaker, and her dispatcher, Paige Henderson, came over the line.

"We have bad news, Chief," Paige started. "Some housecleaners just went to a house on Ocean View Drive to prepare it for an incoming guest. When they got there, they found two dead bodies inside."

Two dead bodies?

Ty didn't like the sound of this.

Especially since it was Cassidy's job to put herself in the middle of things—something that, in the past, had proven to be life-threatening.

CHAPTER SIX

CASSIDY STOOD inside a moderately sized beach house located on the ocean. The place was on the opposite end of the island from where she lived, in the middle of an area primarily filled with rentals.

She stared at the scene in front of her. The man and woman sprawled on the floor were middle-aged, dressed in Hawaiian shirts, and were each probably thirty pounds overweight.

It was bad enough that two people had died here on the island. But making matters worse was the fact that this house was located directly beside the residence the governor had reserved for his vacation.

Coincidence?

Cassidy didn't know yet. But if it was a coincidence, the timing was uncanny.

With more effort than usual, Doc Clemson, who also served as the island's medical examiner, pushed himself to his feet. He'd been kneeling on the floor and examining the bodies in the living room. The storm had cleared about an hour ago, and now sunlight poured into the room, a stark contrast to the death and despair in front of them.

"Cause of death?" Cassidy asked, even though she already had a good idea just based on what she'd observed.

"It looks like a murder-suicide," he stated, trying to catch his breath.

"Why murder-suicide instead of double homicide?" Cassidy asked.

"I'm basing that on past experience, the position of the gun in the man's hand and . . ."

"We found a suicide note," Dillinger said.

Cassidy twisted her head and nodded. "That seems like a good indication. Can I see it?"

Dillinger handed her a piece of paper protected by a plastic bag. She read the words there—words that looked like they'd been crudely written.

Was this a man's handwriting? That's what she would guess based on the lack of elegance.

She'd need to find samples of this guy's writing and compare the two, just to be certain.

Life isn't worth it anymore. There's no reason to go on. Coming to the most beautiful place on earth and ending it all is our only solution. I'm sorry for anyone this hurts.

"He didn't sign his name," Cassidy muttered.

"I thought that was strange also," Dillinger said.

Something about the note didn't sit right with her, but she needed to find out more information about this couple before she drew any conclusions.

"Did you find any IDs?" Cassidy asked.

"Not yet," Dillinger said. "There were no driver's licenses on them, nor have we found any in the house."

"If they're here on vacation, certainly the woman brought a purse and the man brought a wallet."

"Could this be a robbery?"

Cassidy shook her head. "With a suicide note? I don't know."

"We'll keep searching for something to identify them," Dillinger said. "Otherwise, we'll call the rental agency and get information that way."

"Sounds like a plan," Cassidy said. As she stared at the couple, another thought hit her. "Could these people be the girl's parents?"

"I wondered that as well." Doc Clemson stared down at the couple. "I can't rule it out completely, but they would be on the older side to have a girl her age. I'm guessing that these people are in their fifties. It's a possibility, but a little unlikely."

"Grandparents?"

"Maybe."

Cassidy frowned when she studied the couple's faces. "Neither of them really look like her, do they? But that doesn't necessarily mean anything. Children don't always resemble their parents. She could even be adopted."

"There are certainly a lot of variables to contend with," Doc noted.

"But maybe the most obvious clue is the fact that there's no evidence that a child had been staying here," Cassidy said. There are no clothes. No toys. No special snacks or food or cups.

Could these people's deaths have anything to do with Jane Doe?

Cassidy didn't know.

But whatever was going on here on the island, she didn't like it.

CASSIDY STAYED at the scene right up until the time Ty called to let her know Gail had arrived.

Trusting that things were in good hands, Cassidy left to meet Ty at the cottage.

The idea of turning the girl over to a stranger didn't sit well with Cassidy. She knew the procedure and that things like this happened all the time. This was the system that had been put in place.

But the number of unknowns concerning the girl's background and circumstances made caution seize her muscles, her thoughts.

Plus, there was the fact that no one had called about her yet.

One of their theories had been that the girl sneaked out at night while her parents were sleeping. But, if that was the case, then those same parents should be awake by now and have noticed her missing.

Yet no one had reported anything yet.

Cassidy mulled over her thoughts as she drove home. The tension inside her continued to mount as she pulled up, climbed out of the car, and walked up to her cottage.

She paused for a moment to compose herself before going inside.

Drawing in several deep breaths, she glanced at the beach. The ocean looked so peaceful today, almost as if its tirade last night hadn't happened.

She was so blessed to have this oceanfront cottage with Ty. The area where the home was located was rather isolated on the northern end of the island.

This place had belonged to his grandfather at one time until it had been given to Ty. In the past couple of years, Ty had renovated the home, added a second story, and built cabanas out back to house people who came in for his retreats. A salt marsh stretched just beyond the cabanas.

Four times a year, he brought former military here, military who were dealing with hard issues like PTSD, injuries, and broken relationships. He offered them a chance to be renewed and refreshed, gave a listening ear, and brought in counselors to help with concerns. There were also fun aspects included—kayaking, surfing, bonfires.

Her thoughts shifted to the situation at hand.

Did Cassidy have any grounds for keeping the girl here?

Not unless she could prove the girl was in danger.

She might have to take Ty up on his offer to buy time somehow.

With one more deep breath, Cassidy stepped

through her screened porch and walked into her house.

"Cassidy." Gail plastered on a smile as Cassidy paused near the front door.

The woman had been pleasant when Cassidy met her in the past. From what Cassidy remembered, Gail was single and in her mid-thirties, with a stout build and bobbed brown hair.

But right now, for some reason, the woman felt like an enemy.

"Thanks for coming, Gail." Cassidy stopped in front of her and glanced over the woman's shoulders.

Jane Doe sat on the couch, still hugging that ratty pink teddy bear. The forlorn look remained in her gaze. But her eyes moved now. They shot to Cassidy then Gail as if she were nervous or sensed a change was about to take place.

"I guess nobody has come forward to claim her." Gail kept her voice low as she clasped her clipboard to chest.

Cassidy shook her head, also talking quietly. The girl might not have anything to say but that didn't mean she couldn't hear and understand this conversation. "No one. The whole situation is really quite a mystery."

Gail glanced at the girl. "I can't even imagine. She still hasn't spoken a word?"

Cassidy shook her head. "Nothing yet. Maybe she just needs time. Do you have a home set up for her to go to?"

"I do. A nice family over on the mainland. No kids of their own. I think they'll be a good match until we figure out what's going on."

Another wave of defensiveness rose in Cassidy. She wished she could pinpoint exactly why she was feeling this way. But she couldn't.

Cassidy felt Ty's gaze on her. He was reading her body language, wasn't he? He knew she was uncomfortable with this scenario.

But Cassidy needed more time to formulate a viable plan to keep the girl under their protection.

"Gail . . ." Ty stepped closer. "I heard you were a huge movie buff."

Cassidy's eyebrows knit together. Where was he going with this?

"As a matter of fact I am." Gail beamed as if thrilled that Ty knew that about her.

"Specifically, I heard that you really like Navy SEAL movies."

"I love *Act of Valor*," Gail said.

"Funny you say that. My organization is actually

opening their headquarters here on the island. I employ former Navy SEALS. In fact, I have new recruits coming soon. I wondered if you might like to see the facilities?"

Her eyes lit. "Really? Well . . . I shouldn't. I *am* supposed to be working, and we do have a long trip—"

"It won't take that long. It's just a few minutes down the street."

"I'm sure you have other things to do." Gail glanced at Cassidy. "You have to get back to work, right?"

Cassidy smiled. "I don't mind waiting a bit."

"Are you sure?" Gail scrutinized Cassidy's expression a moment.

"I'm positive."

Gail fanned her face and nodded. "Okay then. Navy SEALs, here I come." She giggled and followed Ty outside.

Cassidy welcomed Gail's enthusiastic response. Ty had just bought her at least another hour before a decision had to be made.

She needed to figure out if there was a valid reason for this girl to stay or not.

And time was running out to find those answers.

CHAPTER SEVEN

CASSIDY SAT on the couch next to Jane Doe and offered a friendly smile. The girl stared at her, watching her every move. Cassidy saw the questions in her eyes.

"You're probably wondering who that woman was, aren't you?" Cassidy started. "She's a social worker, and she helps children. She came so she can find you a family to stay with until we find your mom or dad or guardians."

The girl continued to stare but her lips twitched ever-so-slightly.

"We really need to figure out your name now, don't we?" Cassidy continued.

No response, as expected.

Cassidy studied the girl's face. "Hmm . . . I'm thinking . . . Emma. Is your name Emma?"

Nothing registered in the girl's eyes.

"Sarah?"

Still nothing.

"What about Andy. Maybe short for Andrea? I've always thought that would be a great name for a girl."

A blank stare greeted her.

Cassidy leaned back, careful to keep her voice light. "Maybe those names are too short. Maybe you have a longer name. What about Wilhelmina?"

Cassidy couldn't be sure, but she thought she saw a glimmer in the girl's eyes. Not because she'd gotten the name right but because the name was so far off track.

"I'm going to figure out a good name for you," Cassidy said. "Until I do, I need to think of something to call you other than 'the girl.' I don't really love calling you that. But what should I call you?"

The girl stared, almost like she was waiting.

"I know," Cassidy said. "How about if I call you Janie? Kind of a play on Jane Doe but more personal. Would that be okay?"

As expected again, the girl said nothing. But there wasn't a flash of repulsion in her gaze.

"For now, that's what it's going to be." Cassidy nodded, decision made. "Janie. And your teddy bear can be Fuzzy Wuzzy. That's what I called my stuffed animal when I was a kid."

Cassidy's phone rang, and she glanced at the screen. It was Dillinger. She desperately hoped that he had an update for her.

"WE HAVE AN ID ON OUR COUPLE," Dillinger started.

Cassidy rose and paced away from Janie. "What did you find out?"

"Their names are Larry and Linda Taylor," he said. "They're from up near the Richmond, Virginia, area. Larry was fifty-six, and Linda was fifty-four. They have three grown kids, but no grandkids. Best I can tell from their social media, they have no connection with our mystery girl."

"After their children have been informed of their deaths, we can ask the family if anyone recognizes our Jane Doe," Cassidy said quietly.

"Local police will tell them, and I can let you know after that's been done."

"That sounds good. Anything else new?"

"There was one more thing that Doc asked me to tell you."

Cassidy stared at the beach outside, remembering that scene from last night. "What's that?"

"He's rethinking his murder-suicide theory."

"So it looks like," Cassidy glanced back at the girl and lowered her voice, "murder?"

"That's right."

Cassidy's mind raced. "What did these people even do for a living?"

"They owned a bakery in Richmond. It was a small mom and pop type business."

Why would someone target bakery owners?

There had to be something else there.

"Anything unusual about the couple?" Cassidy asked.

"The only other thing I've turned up is that there was some confusion with their rental," Dillinger said. "Another couple was supposed to stay there, but the rental agency accidentally double-booked. I guess things got pretty testy, but the Taylors ended up getting the house and not the other couple."

"What happened to the other renters?"

"They were so angry they refused to go to another home with this particular vacation rental company. I can call the other management companies on the island and see if they decided to rent through one of them instead."

"Do that," Cassidy said. "Let's follow every lead until we figure something out."

"Will do."

She ended the call. She looked over and saw that Janie had appeared beside her.

Janie silently pointed to the beach. Cassidy followed the line of the girl's finger and squinted. Something else had washed up on the shore and now rolled back and forth in the surf.

"Do you want me to go check that out?" Cassidy asked.

The girl's eyes widened and she hugged Cassidy's waist.

Cassidy's gut tightened.

There was no way she was letting this child leave her house.

Not until she knew what had happened to her.

CHAPTER EIGHT

"AND THEN IN that one scene where the SEALs rescued that woman . . ." Gail closed her eyes as a dreamy look swept over her face. "It was just heroic. That's all I can say."

Gail had really enjoyed the tour.

But now they were back at the cottage. As soon as they'd walked in, Ty had seen the tension on Cassidy's face.

Had something happened while he was gone?

The girl had risen from the couch and stood near the window beside Cassidy. Cassidy's arm stretched protectively across her shoulders.

Had Cassidy learned something new about the girl?

His curiosity spiked.

"The tour was absolutely great," Gail said as she stood beside him. Her voice sounded animated and lit with excitement. "Seeing you guys in real life . . ." She patted her heart. "It was on my bucket list, and it was amazing. And not only are you guys handsome, but you're nice too."

Ty shrugged. "What can I say? The outside reflects the inside."

"I could stay here all day and listen to your stories. Can you tell me the one about that helicopter rescue in Egypt again?" She glanced at Cassidy, and her giggle faded. "Well . . . maybe some other time."

"Of course."

"I'm glad you enjoyed your tour," Cassidy said.

"Oh, did I ever." Excitement began to rise in her voice, but Gail closed her mouth, as if trying to tamp it down.

"Ty." Cassidy's voice was lined with tension that only those who knew her well would recognize. "It looks like something washed up on the beach in the distance. Would you mind going to check that out?"

So *that's* what this was about.

"Of course. I'll be right back."

He and Cassidy exchanged a look before he took off in a jog toward the beach.

What else had washed up? Another clue about who this girl might be?

He could only hope so.

He stepped closer and paused. The object appeared to be about two feet long, black, and relatively smooth. The ocean tumbled it back and forth, almost teasing him and daring him to try to reach for it.

As the waves receded, Ty rushed into the surf and grabbed it. His pant legs were the only casualties of the cold ocean water.

As he dropped the object on the ground, Ty saw it was a leather bag.

Kneeling beside it, he used the edge of his T-shirt to touch the zipper, not wanting to smear any potential prints.

Slowly, Ty pulled it open.

Inside, he saw . . . alcohol swabs?

What sense did that make?

Did this have something to do with the girl staying in his cottage?

He wasn't sure if this discovery put his mind at ease or not. Mostly, it just added more questions to an already long list.

AS CASSIDY STOOD in her kitchen waiting for Ty to return, Gail reached her arm toward Janie. "Come here, sweetie."

Janie didn't move.

Gail wiggled her fingers. "I need to get you to the house where you'll be staying before nightfall."

At her words, Janie crept closer to Cassidy and pressed into her. The girl may not talk, but she said plenty.

Gail's gaze softened. "Oh, I can see the two of you have already bonded."

"Gail . . ." Cassidy tried to choose her words carefully. That wasn't to mention the lump in her throat. She wrapped a protective arm around Janie. "How would you feel about Janie staying with me?"

Gail batted her eyelashes in confusion. "Janie? Did she tell you her name?"

Cassidy smiled at the girl beside her. "We came to an agreement that I could call her that until I found out her real name."

Gail cast a quick grin at Janie before looking back up at Cassidy. She lowered her voice before saying, "You know we have an approved list of people who can foster children."

"But these are extenuating circumstances," Cassidy reminded her. "Until we have more answers, I'm not comfortable letting her leave this island."

Gail's smile began to dim. "I'm not sure that's a good idea."

"She could be in danger," Cassidy said just above a whisper. "She needs the protection Ty and I can offer."

"Why would you think she's in danger?" Gail's eyes widened with alarm.

Cassidy glanced at Janie again, wishing she could speak freely. But she needed to be careful what she said in front of the girl.

"Let's just say there have been some other incidents here on the island that have made me very, very cautious. Do you have people on your approved list who can also offer protection?"

"Well . . . no. But I might be able to get an officer stationed outside—"

Cassidy stepped closer and lowered her voice even more. "Look, I know it may not be the traditional route to take. But the fact of the matter is, Ty and I started our application to be foster parents a couple of months ago."

Cassidy had never spoken about that out loud. She and Ty, when they hadn't been able to get pregnant, had decided that maybe foster care was a good option—maybe even fostering with the intent to adopt.

But they'd changed their minds before completing the home study. Ty's work had gotten busy, and Cassidy had revamped several things in the police department. She'd sometimes wondered if things had ultimately worked out the way they were meant to.

Now Cassidy questioned that choice and wished they'd continued.

"I do seem to remember something about that." Gail tilted her head as if gently scrutinizing Cassidy. "But you never went through the entire process."

"I'm hoping we can expedite it," Cassidy said.

"You know I'm not much of a rule bender." Gail let out a nervous laugh.

"I'm not asking you to bend the rules. I'm just asking you to speed them up. You can do a home study right now, can't you?"

"Well . . . that's not usually the way it works."

As Gail's voice turned more rigid, Janie wrapped her arms around Cassidy's waist. It was as if the child was letting Gail know that she wouldn't be leaving easily or without a fight.

Cassidy took that as a sign that this girl really should stay here. Whatever had happened to her,

Janie seemed to view Cassidy and Ty's home as a safe place.

And a safe place was exactly what the girl needed right now. Cassidy would fight with everything in her to give her that safe space.

"You can make some exceptions, right?" Cassidy continued. "Besides, I'm an officer of the law, so I've already had my background checked. Ty was a Navy SEAL. He's gone through all the checks as well."

As Janie squeezed closer to Cassidy, Gail frowned.

She looked back up at Cassidy and shrugged. "Let me see what I can do."

Cassidy released her breath. It was a good start. She just hoped that things worked out in her favor.

Not for Cassidy's sake.

But for Janie's.

CHAPTER NINE

GAIL WANTED to talk to Janie alone for a few minutes. After a moment of hesitation, Cassidy bent toward the girl. She could sense Janie's nerves, her fear over the situation.

Cassidy rubbed Janie's arms and kept her voice soft as she said, "I'll be close if you need anything, okay? Ms. Gail just wants to ask you a few questions."

Janie stared at Cassidy a moment before taking a step back.

Cassidy watched as Gail led Janie to the couch and the two sat down.

Then she stepped onto the porch to talk to Ty. He'd returned from the beach.

Cassidy glanced up at her husband as they stood in front of each other. His brown hair blew in the breeze, revealing his striking blue eyes. His T-shirt showed off his muscles, but not in an arrogant kind of way. Strength was just a way of life for him.

If only she could enjoy the view for a moment.

But she had other things begging for her attention.

"What did you find on the beach?" Cassidy was anxious to hear an update.

"A bag full of alcohol swabs. They're all soaking wet, and you can barely read the labels."

Alcohol swabs? That hadn't been what she was expecting. "What kind of bag were they found in?"

"An old black leather bag."

Cassidy nibbled on her bottom lip as she tried to make sense of things. She'd been desperately hoping for something that might at least give them some direction for this investigation.

"How does that even fit with this whole scenario?" she finally asked.

"That's a great question. I'm not sure yet." Ty crossed his arms and leaned against the wood post beside him. "Remind me what else you found."

"A bag of trash, a piece of wood, and a cooler. We can't even be sure those things are tied with each other or Janie, for that matter."

He let out a long breath before shaking his head. "Nothing seems to fit together, does it? The only good news is that more stuff might wash ashore, stuff that could help us."

"Maybe."

Cassidy's phone buzzed. It was Dillinger again.

She was trying to juggle so many balls right now. She'd been entrusted to care for this community and the people here. She didn't intend to let anybody down. But she did have to remind herself that she was only one person. Her lack of sleep from the night before was beginning to wear on her.

Despite that, she put the phone to her ear. "Dillinger. What's going on?"

"Chief, I was able to track down the other couple who were supposed to stay in that rental house. Their names are Ed and Sandra Ballard."

"Are they still here on the island?"

"I stopped by the new house where they were staying, but they weren't home. However, the management company doesn't have a record of them checking out yet."

"Keep looking into it," Cassidy told him. "I want to know if they know anything."

"Will do."

Cassidy put her phone away and filled Ty in.

He stepped closer, his gaze filled with concern. "Are you doing okay? This is a lot on your shoulders. And on top of everything else that's been going on—"

"I'm fine," she insisted before glancing at her watch. "But, unfortunately, the governor is supposed to arrive on the island in an hour. Mayor Mac wants me there to greet him."

"I'm sure if you called Mac and told him what was going on, he'd understand if you couldn't be there."

"I know. But I need to put my best foot forward for this island. Plus, I need to talk to the governor's security team. I don't think it was a coincidence that the couple who died just happened to be staying in the house right beside Hollick's rental."

"Good point." He lowered his voice. "I wish I could help you."

"You can. By staying here with Janie."

His eyebrows shot up. "Janie?"

Cassidy shrugged. "That's the name I decided we should call her. Long story."

Ty hesitated another moment. "I thought Gail was leaving with her?"

Cassidy quickly explained what had transpired

with Gail and Janie while he was on the beach retrieving the bag of alcohol swabs. "I didn't think you'd mind participating in the home study."

"I'm all in. But do you think Gail is going to be okay with you leaving before we do the home study?"

"You know that little sweet talk thing that you can do when you need to get things done?" Ty didn't use it all the time, but when he needed to be diplomatic, he could pull that side of him out.

"I wouldn't exactly call it sweet talk." Ty shrugged as if offended.

"How about 'the art of being persuasive.' Is that better?"

"Maybe."

"I need you to use that skill now. I need you to let Gail know we'll be great foster parents for this little girl. Maybe she can grant us some type of temporary variance to make it happen. I just need you to work your magic. Besides, she *loves* Navy SEALs." Cassidy patted his solid chest and winked. "You've got this."

Ty glanced back inside where Gail sat beside Janie on the couch. "I'll do my best. And in the meantime, I won't take my eyes off Janie."

"Thank you, Ty. This really means a lot to me."

He planted a firm kiss on her forehead. "For you? Anytime."

CASSIDY QUICKLY FRESHENED up before going to the city offices.

She was right on time. The governor was supposed to arrive via helicopter in twenty minutes. But first she needed to talk to the mayor, Mac MacArthur.

She took a deep breath before knocking on the door to his office.

Her friend was throwing darts at a target positioned across from his desk. He hit the bullseye, looked up, and a smile lit his face when he saw Cassidy.

Mac had been the police chief here on Lantern Beach for years. Another man—Alan Bozeman—had taken over after him for a while, but since he left, Mac had helped show Cassidy the ropes.

The man was constantly trying to hone his skills, going as far as to scale the side of his house, running boot camps for kids in the summer, and even practicing his aim using a dartboard.

"In typical Lantern Beach fashion, I heard that all types of mayhem have broken out," Mac said.

Cassidy lowered herself into the chair across from his desk. "You can say that again."

"I don't like the sound of all this." Mac frowned and twirled a dart between his fingers. "Not just because the governor is coming, but because I don't believe in coincidences."

"Me either—though I have trouble seeing how this girl who washed up might be connected."

"Maybe the girl's not connected. But the dead couple in the house beside the one where Governor Hollick will be staying?" He raised his white eyebrows. "It makes me wonder what's going on."

"To my understanding, nobody else knows the governor is coming here on vacation except for a few members of his staff, right?"

"That's right," Mac said. "Hollick wants to keep this private, especially since so much has been going on in politics right now. He said he needs to get away from the drama."

"Seems understandable."

Mac stood with a sigh. "Are you ready for all the fun to begin? We should probably go so we can meet Hollick at the lighthouse."

The lighthouse had a large open area where helicopters could land on the island.

Cassidy nodded. "Let's get going."

But she knew from experience that the governor's presence here on the island was only going to bring more chaos and confusion to her already strapped department.

They were going to need a divine intervention for everything to go off without a hitch.

CHAPTER TEN

CASSIDY STOOD with her shoulders straight and her posture rigid as Governor Hollick, his wife, and his fourteen-year-old son climbed from the black helicopter.

She stood beside Mac, along with the city manager and one of her officers. Around them, the air swirled as the helicopter propellers turned in fast circles.

Four men flanked the family as they walked toward Mac and Cassidy.

"Chin up, buttercup," Mac muttered.

"Always." Cassidy barely moved her lips, keeping her disposition professional.

Not many people could get away with saying that

to Cassidy, but Mac could. Cassidy practically thought of the man as a father.

One of the security guards surged ahead of the pack and strode toward them. The man wore an earpiece in his ear and a black suit. His square face looked stony, like he hadn't smiled in years.

He briskly walked toward them and extended his hand. "I'm Peter Brinkley, head of security. I talked to the city liaison earlier, but I need to make sure that all the correct security precautions are in place."

They had a city liaison? Cassidy didn't voice the question aloud.

This guy had probably just given Mac's secretary that label.

Cassidy watched as the rest of the entourage bypassed Cassidy and Mac and headed toward a black SUV in the distance.

"First, let me say welcome to Lantern Beach," Cassidy started. "I'm Police Chief Cassidy Chambers. And, of course, you know Mayor Mac MacArthur."

Peter nodded at both of them.

"Earlier today, I had my officers at the house where the governor is staying," Cassidy continued. "We made sure everything there is secure. As well, we've kept the governor's presence here on the island on the down low. Even his name at the rental was under an alias, so no one should know."

"Good," the man said. "And you had the groceries delivered?"

Groceries delivered? What were they? Hired help?

Cassidy clamped her mouth shut.

Mac nodded. "We did. Each of your requests were taken care of."

"Good." Peter's jaw flexed. "And what's this about two dead bodies in the house next to where the governor is staying? Should I be concerned?"

Cassidy pulled up a picture of the couple. "Do you recognize them?"

He studied their faces before shaking his head. "I can't say I do."

"They were from up in Richmond and owned a bakery," Cassidy said. "I didn't find any connection between them and the governor. Plus, neither had a criminal record. Our initial assessment of the scene is that it's a murder-suicide, even though we are continuing to investigate."

Yes, they did have another theory. But it hadn't been fleshed out yet. Besides, there had been a suicide note. There was no need to alarm the governor without cause.

Peter's stone-cold stare became even more icy. "So you don't believe the governor's life is in any danger?"

"That's correct," Cassidy said. "But I assure you that my men and I are on this."

"That's what I like to hear." Peter nodded back to the SUV the governor and his family had climbed into. "They're anxious to get to the house and settle down. It's been a long month."

"I understand," Cassidy said. "If there are any other ways we can be of service to you while the governor is in town, please let us know."

But I won't be bringing you any groceries . . .

"Will do." Peter offered another stiff nod before hurrying back to the SUV. As the vehicle pulled away and the helicopter took off, Cassidy, Mac, and the rest of the gang glanced at each other.

"My feelings are hurt," Mac teased. "Dr. Governor didn't even say hi."

That was what some people called the man. He'd been a physician before going into politics.

Cassidy shook her head, grateful Mac was just joking. "People either love Governor Hollick or hate him. There isn't an in-between. But if that's the way he acts around his constituents . . . I can see why people aren't fans."

"Now we just need to hope that we can keep his presence on the island quiet while he's here," Mac said.

Cassidy had a feeling that would be easier said than done.

But she wasn't going to tell the governor that.

CASSIDY KNEW she didn't have any time to lose, so she headed back to the station.

The good news was that Gail had called. Janie could stay with her and Ty—for a while, at least. If her stay extended into something that was several weeks long, they'd need to take additional steps.

At least, Cassidy could be grateful for that.

She called a meeting of her officers so they could discuss everything that was going on. She started with the protocols that would be in place concerning Governor Hollick. She also had to remind them about the gag order concerning his presence here.

After that, she moved on to the dead couple and the missing renters.

"Has anyone had any luck locating Ed or Sandra Ballard?" Cassidy started.

As everyone shook their heads, Dillinger stepped

forward. “I’ve been monitoring their house, but they haven’t been back.”

“Who’s there now?”

“Banks. He said he hasn’t seen any movement, which makes me wonder if they’ve gone home early. Apparently, it’s not always necessary to officially check out. If you want to leave before the time you’ve paid for is finished, it’s perfectly okay to do that.”

“Then we need to check with people in their hometown and see if they’ve returned home. I want to know what happened to them. Right now, if this wasn’t a murder-suicide, then they’re at the top of my suspect list.”

“Wouldn’t that be the ultimate act of rage? Killing because somebody took your vacation house?” Officer Bradshaw asked. “It seems extreme.”

“That’s true. But I’ve seen crazier things. I want to explore every angle until we can be certain about what happened.”

“That sounds like a good idea,” Bradshaw said. “I’m on it.”

“Any more updates about the murder-suicide?” Cassidy looked at Dillinger again. He’d taken lead on that case.

“I haven’t heard anything from Doc,” he said.

"Last time I talked to him, he told me it would take a while to get the official results back."

"Understood," Cassidy said. "What about the evidence that washed up? Has anyone made any headway on that?"

The men shook their heads.

"It's going to be all-hands-on-deck considering everything that's going on here on the island," Cassidy said. "I just wanted to let you know that our Jane Doe—who's now going by Janie—will be staying with Ty and me until we can find out who her parents are. I want to keep that under wraps. The less people who know, the better. But you need to know also just in case I need you."

"Anything you need, Chief," Dillinger said.

Cassidy nodded. "Great. Now, everybody get to work. We don't have time to waste."

Just as she said the words, the phone rang. It was Ty.

She put the device to her ear, anxious to hear any updates.

"Lisa is bringing some food by for lunch," Ty said. "Have you eaten today?"

"Not yet."

"You have time to come by for long enough to grab a bite?"

Cassidy's first impulse was to say no. But that wasn't the way she wanted to operate. There was nothing wrong with taking a little time to be with her family and to get some nourishment into her.

She glanced at her watch. "I'll be there in ten."

But as soon as she finished eating, she'd head right back here and continue her work.

She had no other choice, not with everything happening here on the island.

CHAPTER ELEVEN

CASSIDY PULLED up to her house at the same time as her friend Lisa Dillinger.

Lisa owned one of Cassidy's favorite restaurants here on the island, a place called The Crazy Chefette. She came up with all kinds of unique food combinations that always kept the taste buds guessing. She was also married to Officer Dillinger.

Cassidy gave her a quick hug when they met in the driveway. "No baby?"

"Skye is babysitting." Skye was another of their friends. She ran a produce stand in-season and had been helping Lisa during the off-season. "She has it easy because Julia was taking a nap when I left."

"She probably can't wait for her to wake up."

Lisa grinned. "Probably. By the way, grab that

bag for me." She nodded to one she'd left on the ground. "I collected some clothes from one of my friends whose daughter has outgrown them. I thought you might need them."

Cassidy lifted the bag. "This is perfect. Thank you."

"No problem."

"How are things going?" Cassidy asked as she and her friend fell into step beside each other, headed toward the front door.

Lisa had her hands full between juggling the restaurant and a newborn.

"They couldn't be better." Lisa practically beamed. "I absolutely love being a mom."

"I knew you would. You just seemed like a natural."

Lisa's smile slipped as she glanced at Cassidy. "And I heard about everything going on with you."

"Just curious, how did you hear?" Cassidy hadn't wanted word to leak on the island about Janie. Not yet.

Lisa frowned. "Braden mentioned it. Is that bad?"

"No, that's what I figured. I just need to keep a pulse on the island scuttlebutt and how many people know. I'd like to keep things under wraps."

Lisa cringed. "Since you mentioned it . . .

everyone on the island is talking about what happened. I'm not sure where or from whom it started. My impression is that there were people who saw officers out searching the beach last night. Serena and Webster were talking about it at the restaurant this morning."

Serena was the resident ice cream lady, news reporter, and all-around interesting character. She was dating Webster Newsome, the island's new newspaper editor.

"How did you know the girl was staying here?" Cassidy slowed her steps and opened the screened porch door for Lisa.

Lisa shrugged and shifted her food to the other hip. "Just because I know you. Now, how about we get inside before your chicken salad with curry and grapes gets warm? Don't worry—I made a few other things and even included some chocolate cake, just in case. I wanted something for everyone."

"That sounds great."

Cassidy wondered how many other people here on the island would assume that Cassidy had the child staying with her. She supposed that would be a good thing. But if this girl's parents *were* looking for her, then it would be easier to track her down.

Another part of her wanted to keep the child's presence a secret.

Maybe that was because of the impending feeling of danger that seemed to hover here on the island.

LISA STAYED LONG ENOUGH to drop off the food and chat for a few minutes before heading back home.

Cassidy and Ty sat at the table with Janie and encouraged her to eat something. She picked up a glass of milk and sipped at it before nibbling on the grilled peanut butter and jelly sandwich Lisa had brought.

It was a good start at least.

"What have you been up to since I left?" Cassidy asked Ty and Janie, trying to keep the conversation light.

Ty grinned at Janie. "We've been doing all kinds of fun things. Haven't we?"

The girl glanced at him but said nothing. Her eyes remained wide but not frightened like they were around other people.

Cassidy's gut told her that the girl felt safe with

her and Ty. And that was the way she intended on keeping it.

"What kind of fun things?" Cassidy continued.

"Let's see, we've been working on a puzzle together," Ty said. "She's pretty good, especially with the edge pieces."

"I can't wait to see what you've put together. I don't have the patience for puzzles."

"That's just because you figure out real life puzzles instead and that takes all your brain energy." Ty winked.

"Maybe you're right. What else have you done?" Cassidy took a bite of her chicken salad.

"After that, we built a tower out of dominos. We got it all the way up to my knees before I accidentally hit it and knocked it down. It crashed everywhere." Ty made motions and sound effects to go with his story.

Cassidy grinned. "It sounds like you made a valiant effort, at least."

"Janie's really good at stacking. Very detail oriented. She even organized all our crayons by color, assorted from the lightest to the darkest."

Cassidy tilted her head. "You sound like one smart girl."

"Oh, she's *definitely* smart."

Even though nothing was normal, a moment of normalcy washed over Cassidy.

How long would this girl stay with them? What if they never found her parents?

Could this girl's presence be some kind of twisted answer to prayer?

Cassidy had so many questions.

As far as she was concerned, Janie could stay with them as long as she needed. Having a child in her home . . . it was what she'd been praying for.

Cassidy shook those thoughts aside.

Right now, Cassidy needed to tap into some of that patience she'd mentioned earlier—the same patience needed to put a puzzle together—the patience she sometimes lacked. She could use some in this situation.

As she ate the last bite of her soup, her phone rang.

It was Bradshaw. She excused herself before answering.

"Chief, you're going to want to get down to the station," Bradshaw said. "A couple is here claiming to be Janie's parents."

CHAPTER TWELVE

AS SOON AS Cassidy pulled up to the station, Bradshaw met her outside. "Thanks for coming so quickly."

She tucked a stray hair back into her bun and paused before she headed into the station. "What do you know about these people so far?"

"They said they're from the Baltimore area," Bradshaw said. "The family was taking a boat trip down the Intracoastal Waterway. They said their six-year-old daughter is mildly autistic and, while they were sleeping, she must have put on the life jacket and jumped overboard."

Cassidy mentally calculated everything she was learning. So far, their story could be true, she supposed.

So why was she feeling skeptical?

"Where are they now?" Cassidy asked.

"They're in your office. Dillinger is outside the door, keeping an eye on them—just in case."

"Did you get a read on them?"

Bradshaw shrugged. "Hard to say. They seemed worried. Seemed nice enough. Nothing raised any red flags. Why do you seem cynical?"

"I don't know. Of course, I want the girl to find her parents. But the fact that she can't talk makes everything a little more complicated."

"I understand." He nodded and waited for her next order. "What do you need me to do?"

"While I'm in there talking to them, I'll get their driver's licenses. I want you to run background checks on them. I want to know as much about these people as I can before I hand their child back over to them—*if* Janie is their child."

"Will do, Chief."

Cassidy sucked in a deep breath and straightened her shirt before approaching her office. She dismissed Dillinger with a nod, plastered on a smile and entered the room.

"Good afternoon," she started. "I'm Police Chief Cassidy Chambers. I'm sorry that I kept you waiting."

"I'm Kate Donovan, and this is my husband, Rick."

The two people sitting in front of her desk appeared to be in their early thirties. The woman was pretty, with dark hair and a slim build. The man looked like the professional type with his short-sleeve button-up shirt and designer jeans. He had blond hair that was thinning and cut short.

But it wasn't as much what they looked like that made Cassidy take notice. It was how they were acting.

Their features seemed tight, squeezed. Their motions were quick. They looked worried.

That should set her at ease.

So why didn't it?

Cassidy lowered herself across from them at her desk. "As per protocol, I'm going to need to get your licenses so we can handle everything through the correct legal procedures."

"Where is Annabeth?" The woman leaned forward so far that she practically lunged from her seat. "I need to see my daughter."

"We can bring her here soon. She's resting now, and we have paperwork to figure out first." A slight tinge of guilt filled Cassidy at her words.

If these people truly were Annabeth's parents, it

was downright mean to keep them from their daughter after everything that had happened.

But Cassidy had to cross all her T's and dot all her I's.

The girl's protection was her first priority.

The man and woman pulled out their licenses and handed them to Cassidy. She strode to the door and handed them to Bradshaw, who now lingered near the reception desk. He gave her a nod, silently communicating that he knew just what to do.

Then Cassidy strode back into her office and shut the door. "I'm going to need you to tell me exactly what happened."

"Why?" Kate's voice climbed with surprise. "Why is it important? We just want our daughter back. Why are you keeping her from us?"

"I'm sorry, ma'am." Cassidy used her most reassuring voice, trying to set them at ease. "This is just procedure. I promise you the girl is doing just fine."

"I don't understand why you would have a protocol like this." Rick's face began to redden. "Isn't the most important thing that we reunite with our daughter?"

Cassidy raised her hand, trying to get them to calm down before the situation bubbled out of control. "Of course. Of course. Please, don't get me wrong. Ever since we found Annabeth—you said that was her name?—her safety has been our first priority. Now, instead of talking too much about this, how about if we go ahead with this paperwork?"

Kate leaned back, still looking ill at ease. The man, however, was stiff and on the edge of his seat as if he wanted to spring to his feet and make more demands.

"What do you need to know?" Kate asked. "We've been through all this with one of your officers."

"Yes, and I greatly appreciate your patience with this." Cassidy needed more details. She needed for things to fall in place. "Now, can we start at the beginning?"

THE BEGINNING of Rick and Kate's story matched with what Bradshaw had told Cassidy.

She listened anyway, wanting to hear each detail for herself. Plus, it wasn't only their words she wanted to hear. She wanted to watch their body language also.

Cassidy wasn't sure what it was about these two that made her not trust them. But she needed to remain objective. Just because she had a personal connection with Janie, she couldn't let that cloud her judgment.

She hadn't realized this would be as hard as it was.

Rick softened his shoulders, a hint of remorse washing over his features. "I should have paid more attention to what was happening. But we were all sleeping. When we woke up this morning, Annabeth was gone."

"What kind of boat were you on?"

"It's a twenty-five-foot cabin cruiser."

"Where were you on the water when this happened?" Cassidy grabbed a map from her drawer and spread it over her desk, silently indicating to them that they should point out the exact area.

The man leaned forward and glanced at the map for what felt like a little too long to be a seasoned waterman. Finally, he pointed to an area of water right outside of Lantern Beach.

"Here," he said. "We were around this area."

"So you veered off the Intracoastal Waterway and into the ocean?" What sense did that make? The ocean was far more treacherous.

Kate's eyes shifted to the left as she sheepishly shrugged. "We thought we could handle it. Rick is a fairly seasoned waterman. He took trips with his parents ever since he could walk."

"But that was the night it stormed so badly. How does a small boat like yours hold up during a storm like that?"

Rick and Kate exchanged glances.

"It was rough," Rick finally said. "But we made it through."

"I'm surprised you were resting at all," Cassidy continued. "I would imagine it would be hard to sleep."

Kate's throat visibly tightened. "It was difficult, but we managed. We were more concerned with keeping the boat afloat than maybe we should have been. I didn't even think to check to see if Annabeth was still there."

"And does Annabeth have any past issues with running away?"

Rick and Kate exchanged another glance.

"As a matter of fact, yes, she does," Rick said. "As I mentioned to your officer, she's mildly autistic. But we never guessed that she would jump overboard."

"Why is that?"

"Because she hates water," Kate quickly asserted.

Cassidy twisted her neck in confusion. "So why did you take Annabeth out on a boat if she hates water so much? That doesn't seem like it would be healthy for her, especially with her challenges."

Rick's face reddened. "Why are you treating us like we're suspects here? We only came to get our daughter. And now you're keeping her from us."

He sprang to his feet and leered at Cassidy.

"I need you to calm down," Cassidy said. "I know the situation is difficult."

He placed his fists on her desk as he leaned closer. "You don't know the beginning of difficult."

CHAPTER THIRTEEN

"MR. DONOVAN." Cassidy's jaw clenched. "Sit down. Please."

Kate touched his arm, and his shoulders seemed to loosen. Hesitantly, he sat back in his chair.

Cassidy gave him a moment to get himself under control.

Finally, he shrugged as if mentally trying to dislodge his negative thoughts. "Sorry about that. I'm just a little worked up. I miss my little girl."

"I understand. Not much longer."

But some things still weren't making sense for Cassidy.

Like why would they take a child who was afraid of water on such a long trip? Why turn to the ocean with the storm coming? And if the water was as rough as forecasters said it was, why wouldn't someone check on their daughter in the middle of everything?

Cassidy still had even more questions she hoped they could answer.

"So now, where were we?" Cassidy continued. "It was storming, and you guys were trying to keep the boat afloat in the ocean. There were some pretty big waves out there, weren't there? I heard they were getting up to twelve feet."

Kate's expression became even more pinched. "It was quite scary, something I don't ever want to experience again."

Then why had Rick said earlier that they had all been sleeping and that, when they'd woken up, they'd noticed their daughter was missing?

Cassidy didn't know much about boating, but in a vessel that size, she'd imagine that the beds were in the same room—which would make it more noticeable if their daughter was missing.

More things didn't make sense to her.

"The life jacket that she was found in . . ." Cassidy glanced at both of them, watching their expressions to see if either of them showed a spark of recognition at the mention of it.

"What about it?" Rick asked.

"I'm curious about why my name was written on the bottom of it."

Rick's face went pale. He'd had no idea her name was there.

That realization made Cassidy's suspicions rise even more.

AFTER A MOMENT OF SILENCE, Rick Donovan finally shook his head. His gaze held a perplexed look that seemed sincere.

"I can't tell you the answer to that question," he said. "I . . . I have no idea, and I have no good guesses."

"Had either of you even heard of me before today?" Cassidy asked.

"No, I can't say that we have. But you know . . ." Kate paused for long enough to purse her lips in thought. "We did buy some used life jackets from somebody in Manteo. Is there any possible reason they might have had your name on one of them, and we just didn't notice when we purchased them?"

Interesting . . . "I can't think of any reason why my name would be on one. As far as I know, no one has ever labeled one for me personally—especially not one intended for a child. Can I have the name of that person that you purchased those from down in Manteo?"

"It was a man that we met at the harbor." Rick tapped his lip. "We realized that Annabeth was over the weight limit for the life jacket that we had, so we wanted to buy a new one for her. It just so happened that he was going to get rid of his, and we made a deal."

"And you don't remember anything else about him?"

Rick shrugged. "That's correct. I'm sorry. I should have paid more attention."

Convenient . . .

"Can I see any pictures that you might have of Annabeth?" Cassidy asked.

If these people were her parents, they should have plenty of photos of their daughter.

"Of course." Kate fumbled on her phone until she finally offered a small smile at whatever she saw on her screen.

Cassidy's heart lurched in her throat as Mrs. Donovan handed her the cell. Pictures filled the screen. Pictures of Janie.

Or Annabeth, she should say.

There was no denying it was the same girl.

In each photo, Annabeth was smiling, happy.

In one photo, the girl held a dandelion beneath her nose. In another, she hung from some monkey bars at a park.

But one thing was missing.

Pictures of Rick and Kate Donovan with Annabeth.

Cassidy glanced up at the couple. “You don’t have any pictures of the three of you together? A family portrait maybe?”

Kate shook her head, maybe a little too quickly. “I hate having my photo taken.”

“I understand.” Cassidy still needed to make them think that she was on their side. “I don’t like having my photo taken either.”

Before the two of them could say anything else and before Cassidy could ask them about Annabeth’s inability to speak, someone knocked at the door.

Bradshaw.

“Can I have a moment with you?” he asked Cassidy.

“Of course.” Cassidy glanced back at the couple. “If you’ll excuse me for just a moment, I’ll be right back.”

Based on the look on Bradshaw's face, he had something important to tell her.

Was it about this couple's background check?

If there was anything fishy there, they needed to discover it now. Because, as of this moment, Cassidy had no viable reason not to bring Annabeth to the station for a reunion.

CHAPTER FOURTEEN

BRADSHAW NODDED toward the space at the end of the hallway, farther away from Cassidy's office.

Cassidy's curiosity grew. "What's going on?"

"I just ran these people's driver's licenses," Bradshaw started. "At first, I got a hit on who they were. But then I started to dig deeper. It turns out that Rick and Kate Donovan died in a car wreck two years ago."

Cassidy's spine straightened. "What do you mean? Do they even have a daughter?"

"They did have a daughter named Annabeth, and the girl looks similar to the child we found on the beach. But not exactly."

She frowned. "I knew something was fishy about their story. Who in their right mind would veer from the Intracoastal Waterway in a twenty-five-foot boat with a major storm coming? I don't know a lot about boating, but don't seasoned watermen usually recommend a boat that's at least thirty foot if people are in the ocean?"

"They do," Bradshaw said. "I agree that it sounds suspicious. I can keep looking for more information . . ."

Cassidy shook her head. "I'm not sure what else you're going to find. It looks like these two have assumed other people's identities and hoped we'd fall for it."

"Why would they do that?" Bradshaw stared at Cassidy as if she held the answers.

Cassidy's jaw stiffened. "I don't know. But they want this girl for some reason."

"I don't like the sound of that."

"Me either."

"So what are you going to do now?"

"I'm going to go in there and talk to them and get to the bottom of this," Cassidy said. "And they are not going to leave here until we have some answers."

"Do you need me to go in there with you?"

"How about if you wait by the door instead?"

"Of course." He offered a nod.

Cassidy had always appreciated his dedication.

Apprehension built in her as she walked back to her office and twisted the knob.

But when she opened the door, the seats across from her desk were empty and her window was open.

The Donovans were gone.

"WE'VE GOT TO FIND THEM!" Cassidy charged toward the back door. "Bradshaw, get Banks and Dillinger to help you."

Cassidy darted outside and glanced around the fenced-in area behind the police station.

It was empty.

Where had those people gone? They couldn't have gotten but so far.

Knowing she didn't have any time to lose, she dashed back inside and out the front door.

As she did, she spotted a black sedan speeding away in the distance.

That had to be them.

Bradshaw appeared beside her, keys in his hands.

Without a word, they climbed into his squad car, turned on the siren, and sped down the road.

But that thirty seconds had given the Donovans just enough time to get a head start.

As Cassidy searched the street in front of her, she didn't see their car. Had they turned off onto one of these side roads?

She would search every street if she had to.

"Go faster," she told Bradshaw.

He pressed harder on the accelerator.

As he did, a car pulled from one of the gravel lanes out in front of them, suitcases loaded on top and four bicycles teetering on a rack on the back.

Bradshaw braked and flashed his lights, urging them to move out of the way. But the driver clearly had nowhere to go. A ditch stretched on one side, and cars zoomed past on the other.

Meanwhile, the vehicle could only move so fast with everything loaded onto it. Cassidy would guess a family was inside—a family with young children, based on the bikes. Children who may have distracted the driver when he'd pulled out.

"Come on!" Cassidy tried to hold back her frustration. But she needed to know who that couple really was who'd run from the station. So much hinged on finding answers.

Finally, the tourist car pulled onto another side street, and Cassidy and Bradshaw sped past.

But it was too late.

The Donovans' car was nowhere to be seen.

But it had to be here on this island somewhere. There was no bridge to leave this place, only ferries and boats.

And Cassidy would search every inch of this island if she had to.

CHAPTER FIFTEEN

CASSIDY AND BRADSHAW had driven up and down every road between the station and the south end of the island—twice.

The black sedan was nowhere to be seen.

Frustration built in her until she felt as if she could explode.

That wasn't acceptable. That vehicle *had* to be around here somewhere.

"Head toward the lighthouse," she told Bradshaw. "My mind keeps going back to that area."

That was the direction they'd been heading during the chase. She supposed it was a possibility that the vehicle hadn't pulled down a side street.

Maybe it had kept going.

As they pulled closer to the area where the

island's trademark lighthouse was located, Cassidy instructed Bradshaw to slow down.

She scanned everything around her. The entrance to the area was wooded and fairly secluded.

The perfect hideout.

Was this where the Donovans had come?

She pointed to a clearing between the trees. "Pull in there. I'm going to check this on foot if I have to."

"Yes, Chief."

Bradshaw drove into the foliage as far as he could before putting the car in Park.

Cautiously, Cassidy climbed out. Her hand remained near her gun in case trouble was waiting for them.

Based on the way the grass had been matted in the area, someone had come this way recently.

The Donovans?

Maybe.

Or it could have been some teens wanting privacy for partying or making out.

With Bradshaw beside her, she followed the track of flattened grass.

She froze as something caught her eye.

Fresh, broken branches.

Branches that had been placed over a car as someone had quickly tried to conceal it.

Cassidy pushed the foliage away and frowned.

This was it.

The Donovans' car.

They had ditched it here.

She froze as she glanced around, listening for any signs of them.

In her gut, she knew they were gone.

Still, she had to be certain.

She studied the ground and spotted more grass that had been pushed down, most likely by feet treading through the area. She followed the trail.

It ended at the beach.

She rushed onto the sand, looking for any signs of the couple.

But as she saw a boat pulling from the shore, she knew the Donovans were inside.

They'd had a backup plan this whole time.

She grabbed her phone and put in a call to the Coast Guard.

Maybe they could catch them.

She hoped.

In the meantime, Cassidy was going to look inside the car and see if she could find any clues about these people's real identities.

She didn't have high hopes, but maybe—just maybe—something had been left behind. She'd have the vehicle towed to the station so they could properly examine it.

But before she did that, she needed to make a call to Ty.

She needed to let him know what was going on so that he could keep an eye on Janie—or Annabeth. Was that even the girl's real name?

Things were even more dire now than they had ever been.

BACK AT THE station an hour later, the crew met in the conference room so each officer could give an update on their cases.

"The car the Donovans were driving was stolen from Manteo earlier today." Banks stared at a piece of paper in his hands, probably a report he'd gotten from a neighboring police department.

He'd run the plates for Cassidy.

"We have it on camera that the couple came over on a ferry this morning," Banks continued. "They arrived on the island a good four hours before they showed up at the police station."

Four hours? Not that Cassidy had any doubts, but if they'd truly been Annabeth's parents, there was no way they'd wait four hours before coming in.

"When they realized I was suspicious of them, they got spooked and fled. But their plan was to take Annabeth and leave with her." Cassidy paced the floor, her gut clenching with each step. "The question is why. *Why* do these people want this girl so badly that they would risk so much and go through all this trouble?"

"Maybe she's an heir to a fortune." Bradshaw crossed his arms as he stood near the door.

"I suppose that's a possibility," Cassidy said. "But if that's the case, I'm surprised her parents haven't put out a plea for people to locate her."

"Maybe she's from another country and she was trafficked in on a boat," Dillinger said.

"Another possibility that perhaps we should explore," Cassidy said. "But what would make this little six-year-old girl so valuable that someone would go through all this trouble?"

"Human trafficking is a very profitable business," Bradshaw said. "Much more profitable than dealing drugs. Drugs? You use them once and they're gone. Humans can be used over and over again. It's a sad reality."

Cassidy's stomach roiled. Even though she

already knew those facts, the reminder made indignation rise in her. All injustices were wrong. But some were just deplorable.

"Anybody else have any other possibilities that you want to throw out?" She stared at each of her officers.

They stared back, the same look of determination in their gazes. They didn't want these people to get away with anything either.

Cassidy had already talked to Ty and told him to keep an eye on Janie. That's what Cassidy had decided to call her, despite the name the Donovans had given.

Besides, they'd run Annabeth's name through a system, and there hadn't been any hits.

"The couple clearly had pictures of this girl from another time." Cassidy remembered her conversation with the man and woman. "I can't be certain, of course, but the photos didn't appear to be Photoshopped."

"Do you remember anything distinctive about the images?" Bradshaw asked. "Anything that might show where this girl has been or where she lived? Did it look like she was in a foreign country?"

Cassidy frowned as she pictured each one of the shots. "That wasn't my impression when I saw them.

In the photos, she looked happy and well-adjusted. She wore nice clothes, and her hair was neat. In one picture, she was holding a dandelion and there was lush green grass behind her. In another photo, she hung from some monkey bars."

"Like at a playground?" Banks asked.

"Maybe a playground, but I didn't see other kids in the background. I'm inclined to say it was a backyard."

"So maybe she does come from a wealthy family," Banks said.

"It's a definite possibility that money is a motivator here," Cassidy said.

"Chief, what do you think these people's end game was?" Dillinger asked. "Let's say you had taken them at their word and handed this girl over to them. Did they actually think she'd go?"

"I have a feeling that's why they told me she was mildly autistic," Cassidy said. "My guess is that they were going to claim that's why she might refuse to go with them or might act frightened."

Dillinger frowned. "They seemed to think of everything."

Yes, they had. And that's what scared Cassidy the most.

CHAPTER SIXTEEN

TY LOOKED up when he heard the door open. He'd already glanced out the window when he heard tires outside the cottage. Cassidy was back home earlier than he'd thought she would be, considering everything going on.

He rose to meet her and planted a kiss on her cheek. "You're home."

She nodded, her gaze switching from Ty to Janie. "I wanted to check on everyone."

"Everything is fine here," Ty said. "Janie has been busy drawing."

"Coloring?" Cassidy's eyebrows shot up. "Any interesting pictures?"

"There are some," Ty said. "Maybe she'd like to show them to you."

"I would love that."

Cassidy walked toward the couch where Janie sat. Cassidy seated herself on one side of the girl and Ty sat on the other. They both bent toward the coffee table where the pictures were scattered.

"Can I see some of your artwork?" Cassidy asked.

Janie said nothing, just looked at the pictures and seemed to give silent approval.

Cassidy began to sort through them. Ty watched as she did, interested to hear her thoughts.

Some of the pictures were just flowers, trees, and hearts. Many appeared to be mindless scribble. But there were a few . . .

Cassidy paused at one of them that had caught Ty's eye. It was a picture of three stick figures. From all appearances, the images appeared to be a man, woman, and a child.

Was this Janie's family?

That had been Ty's first thought when he'd seen it.

"Is this your mom and dad?" Cassidy pointed to the picture.

The girl stared back at Cassidy with the same wide-eyed expression but said nothing, just as Ty had expected she might.

Cassidy's gaze went to the other pictures.

Certainly, she had to be wondering if there were any other clues there.

Maybe there were. Or maybe if Janie continued to draw, there would be eventually.

Ty glanced at Cassidy again and felt a surge of worry wash through him. She was good at her job. Almost too good. So good that she got wrapped up in cases until she saw them to completion.

The last time he had seen Cassidy look this tired was when terrorists had hidden an EMP on the island.

Either way, he worried about her. She'd made tremendous strides with her small department, but sometimes he couldn't help but think Cassidy needed even more people on duty, especially at times like these.

Cassidy cleared her throat and turned to Janie. Ty knew she was about to say something significant. But what?

"I want to show you something," Cassidy started. "If I pull up a picture on my phone, can you tell me if you recognize the people?"

Janie remained quiet.

As Cassidy pulled out her phone, Ty anxiously waited to see what she'd discovered.

Did she have a lead? And, if so, what did that

mean for this precious little girl who was in their care?

AT THE STATION EARLIER, Cassidy had taken pictures of the Donovans' driver's licenses and cropped the photos so that only their headshots could be seen.

She'd questioned whether it was a good idea or not to show Janie these photos. But if she didn't, she might be missing a good opportunity to find answers—and answers would help keep Janie safe.

Cassidy only wished the girl could speak. That some of the light would return to her eyes—light like Cassidy had seen in those photos of her.

First, they had to get through the hard stuff.

Cassidy found a picture of the man and held the phone out toward Janie. "Do you know who this man is?"

Janie's eyes widened at the photo, and she froze, barely breathing.

She *definitely* reacted to the photo, which led Cassidy to believe Janie *had* seen that man before. Had he hurt her? Hurt her parents?

Cassidy wasn't comfortable with either of those ideas.

Despite her hesitation, Cassidy swiped to the left. She showed Janie a picture of the woman this time, the supposed Kate Donovan. "I know this might be hard. But how about her? Have you seen this woman before?"

That same frozen expression remained on the girl's face, and her breaths seemed to become even more shallow.

She'd definitely seen these people before. If only Cassidy could get some information out of her . . .

But she didn't want to push the girl too hard. Besides, until they could figure out a way to get her to communicate, conversations like this wouldn't get them very far. All Cassidy could rely on was the girl's body language.

Or maybe she should call in a child psychologist. Maybe someone with more training could get more information from Janie. Maybe they could use art to decipher what was in Janie's brain.

Cassidy kept that idea in the back of her mind. It could be worth exploring.

Just then, trembles overtook Janie.

Maybe Cassidy had already pushed the girl too far.

Cassidy exchanged a look with Ty before putting her arm around the girl.

The next thing she knew, the child buried herself in Cassidy's arms.

She didn't cry. She didn't say anything.

But the girl was obviously terrified.

Her reaction only confirmed that something terrible was going on.

"It's okay, sweetie," Cassidy murmured. "Those people won't hurt you anymore. You'll be safe here with us."

Nothing would change Cassidy's mind about that.

CHAPTER SEVENTEEN

CASSIDY WISHED she could take away the girl's pain and fear. But all she could do was hold her.

As she did, an ache formed in her chest. Cassidy desperately wanted a child of her own to hold in her arms.

Would she ever get that opportunity? Would God ever grant her that gift? Could she seriously consider adoption?

She knew it was a possibility. But Cassidy longed to know the feeling of having a baby growing inside her. She hadn't even realized how much she longed for a child until that possibility seemed to be stripped away.

As tears began to pool in her eyes, she pushed

those thoughts aside. She had other things she needed to concentrate on at the moment.

Starting with the fact that she was no closer to finding answers about what had happened to Janie than she was before. Not really.

Sure, that man and woman had come in. Cassidy did have their photos, and she was circulating them to other police departments in the area. But, other than that, she had no leads. Only more questions.

She thought through the theories that her officers had thrown out to her. Could this girl be a victim of human trafficking? Could she be some type of heiress to a fortune?

Cassidy had no idea. They had no hits on the girl's photo yet—they were still running it through an online search. Part of Cassidy just wanted to pull that information and give this girl some privacy.

But given the dynamics of the case that didn't seem like a viable option.

Instead, she pressed a kiss to the girl's head. Part of her wished she could just stay here with Janie all day. But she had a job to do, and that job required finding answers.

Her phone rang, and Cassidy saw that it was Mac.

With Janie still in her arms, she put the device to her ear. "Hey, Mac. What's going on?"

"Peter—the head of security for the governor—has asked if you could meet him at the governor's place."

A pinch of irritation started at her spine. "Pertaining to work?"

"He won't tell me. He said it was a security matter and that the less people who knew the details, the better. I know you're juggling a lot right now, Cassidy . . ."

"No, I'll go. I'll see what he wants."

"You sure?"

She squeezed Janie a little harder. "It's no problem. I'll keep you updated . . . if I can."

"COME AGAIN?" Cassidy said as she stared at Peter.

She stood in the entry to the governor's rental house. Peter had pulled her inside, appearing as if he had a bone to pick with her. His gruff tone had immediately set her on edge.

"Why do you have someone patrolling past the house?" Peter stared at her, his gaze unyielding and full of accusation.

Cassidy had to keep her response in check—and not stoop to his level. "I don't have any of my guys driving past your house. Why would you ask that?"

"Because an unmarked black police SUV has gone past the house every hour or so all morning."

Cassidy's shoulders tightened as she heard his words. Black vehicle? Like the one the Donovans had driven?

"It's not one of my guys," Cassidy told him. "If you'd called me when you spotted the vehicle, I could have sent one of my officers out here to check it out."

His gaze narrowed, as if he didn't like that response.

"Did you follow this person?" Cassidy continued. "Get their plate number?"

His eyes remained stony. "There was a type of cover over the license plate, so I couldn't read it. I did run outside and try to chase the guy once. But the driver pulled away before I caught him."

Cassidy forced herself to remain respectful as she processed what he told her. "Why did you think the vehicle was an unmarked police car?"

"It was my impression of the car."

This guy had clearly never worked in law

enforcement. He was making entirely too many assumptions.

"Even if it had been an unmarked police car, I'd think that offering extra manpower to keep Governor Hollick safe would be a positive. Instead, you called me out of an important meeting to chew me out about this?"

That was what irritated her the most.

Her words didn't seem to faze him. "I'm handling security, and the less attention we can draw to this house, the better. People notice things like cars patrolling an area."

Just then, realization dawned on Cassidy. There was more to this than what met the eye. "Is there something I should be concerned about? Is something going on with the governor that should cause me to devote extra manpower for his stay here?"

Something flickered in Peter's gaze before quickly disappearing. "That's not necessary. As I said, my team and I can handle it."

"If you can handle it, then why did you call me over here?"

His eyes narrowed even more, and the muscles along his neck tightened. "That's all I'll be needing from you."

Cassidy's gaze wandered behind him, and she

saw Governor Hollick with his family in the living room. They were gathered playing some type of game at the coffee table.

They talked to each other in low, subdued tones —very much unlike the rowdy game nights Ty and Cassidy usually had at their place.

Another guard was stationed near the kitchen. He gazed out the window, almost as if watching for trouble to arrive.

Interesting.

Did the governor always travel with four members on his security team? It seemed like overkill to Cassidy. Then again, what did she know?

Either way, it was obvious that she wasn't going to be getting any more information from Peter today.

She turned toward the door. "Have a great afternoon."

She felt his icy gaze on her as she left.

There was definitely more going on here with the governor than met the eye.

The question was, what?

CHAPTER EIGHTEEN

CASSIDY WENT BACK to the station for a few more hours before heading home to get some shut-eye. She'd be no good to anyone if she didn't get some sleep tonight—at least a few hours. She could handle the occasional all-nighter, but rest was important.

That's what her doctor had told her also. If she ever wanted to get pregnant, it was important that she take care of herself—manage her stress, eat balanced meals, get plenty of exercise.

Stress management could get challenging sometimes here on the island.

Ty, as usual, met her at the door with a kiss. As Cassidy glanced behind him, she didn't see Janie anywhere.

"She's asleep," Ty said. "After you showed her those pictures, she seemed exhausted. We ate some soup, and then, when I asked her if she was ready to go to bed, she walked toward her room. I just checked on her, and she's snoozing."

"I keep wondering if it was a mistake to show her those photos." Cassidy left her jacket and keys near the door and stepped toward the fireplace.

She hadn't realized how chilled she was. When the sun had set, the temperature had probably dropped fifteen degrees.

"At least now we know that these people have some connection to her—although I have no idea what it might be." Ty walked with her to the couch, grabbing a plate on the way past. "I made you a sandwich. Figured you'd be hungry."

"Thank you. I could eat, now that you mention it. I'm just sorry we couldn't eat together."

"You have a lot going on right now."

Cassidy took a bite of her ham and cheese, letting the flavors wash over her tastebuds. Ty had always been an excellent cook—even when it came to something simple like a sandwich. Something about his added touches made everything taste better.

After she swallowed, she said, "I've been trying to

figure out those connections all day. We've thrown out a lot of theories, but we still don't have any answers. We even went as far as to see if she could be royalty of some sort. Best we can tell, she's not."

"We don't even know if she's American," Ty said.

"No, we don't. But she seems to understand English."

"I agree. But we still have a lot to figure out here, don't we?"

Cassidy sighed. "Thank you for taking care of her. I know that you have a lot going on too with the new recruits coming in for Blackout."

"Colton is taking care of a lot of those details. But at some point tomorrow, I'll need to stop in at the headquarters to check things out. I was wondering about how you would feel if Elise or Bethany kept an eye on Janie for a little while. I could have them bring either Colton or Griff as an extra security precaution."

"I'm sure that both of those ladies would be great with Janie. I totally understand. If I can't be here with Janie, we can do that. I would bring her with me into work, but I feel like the less people who see her out in public, the better. As far as I know, only a handful of people know she's staying with us. I'd love to keep it that way."

"Understood." Ty studied her face a moment. "You look tired."

"I am. I'm hoping that once I get some sleep, maybe I'll be able to think more clearly."

Before they could say another word, a bloodcurdling scream split the air.

And it came from the direction of Janie's bedroom.

TY CHARGED down the hallway toward Janie's room.

Something was wrong.

Was she having nightmare? Or was it something more sinister?

Given everything that had been going on, he couldn't be sure.

He threw the door open to her room, Cassidy and Kujo on his heels.

As he charged inside, he saw Janie curled up in bed with the blankets up to her neck. Her wide eyes were fastened on the window.

Ty glanced that way just in time to see a shadow there.

Someone was outside his home.

"Stay here!" he yelled. "Kujo, on guard!"

The dog sat at attention by the door. No one would get past him—no one except Ty.

Most things Cassidy could handle. But Ty was taking on this one himself.

He sprinted from the room and through the cottage until he was outside.

As he reached his driveway, he spotted a figure disappearing down the road.

Ty wasn't going to let him get away that easily.

He took off in a run after the intruder.

Ty was fast, but this guy had a head start.

Still, Ty wouldn't give up.

Whoever had been peering in the window *had* to have some type of involvement in this case. If Ty was able to catch him, maybe they'd have some answers they desperately needed.

He pushed himself to go faster as he headed down the gravel lane.

When he was only twenty feet away from the man, a black SUV screeched to a halt at the end of the lane.

The front passenger-side door flung open, and the man jumped inside the vehicle in time for the SUV to squeal away, leaving a cloud of dust behind it.

Ty kept running until he reached the street.

His gaze trailed the vehicle, and he squinted, trying to make out the license plate.

But it was no use. It was too dark.

His hands went to his hips as he sucked in deep breaths and watched the SUV disappear.

Cassidy needed to get her officers out there to search for these people.

Ty only hoped that it wasn't too late to catch them.

CHAPTER NINETEEN

CASSIDY GLANCED up as Ty walked into Janie's room. She'd been sitting beside the girl, an arm around her, anxiously waiting for Ty to return.

Air whooshed from her lungs.

Ty was okay. *Praise God.*

Had he caught this guy?

Based on the stony look on his face, she'd guess the answer was no.

Ty offered a subtle headshake to let Cassidy know her suspicions were correct. The guy had gotten away.

She bit back a frown.

She *really* wanted a moment alone to talk to him. But she couldn't leave Janie alone, not after what had just happened.

The girl had been so scared she'd actually wet the bed.

Cassidy turned to the girl. "Why don't we go to the bathroom to get you cleaned up? In the meantime, Ty can change the sheets for us."

Ty nodded. "I'd be happy to."

Cassidy kept an arm around Janie as they stood and headed toward the hallway. As she passed Ty, she paused and lowered her voice. "What happened?"

"A SUV picked him up at the end of the lane before I could get to him."

Had that vehicle been waiting in case the guy grabbed Janie? Was he supposed to take the child and run?

The thought of it caused bile to rise inside her.

Her gaze met Ty's, and she continued to keep her voice quiet. "Could you make out anything about him?"

Ty shook his head, his lips pressed together in disappointment. "Unfortunately, he was wearing all dark clothing."

"How about the SUV?"

"It was black, and I couldn't read the license plate."

A frown tugged at her lips. "That sounds like the

same SUV that's been patrolling past the governor's place."

"Isn't that interesting?"

"Yes, it is. Banks is out looking for that vehicle now. Maybe if we're lucky, he'll be able to find it."

"Let's hope."

She took another step away when another question leaked out. "How did somebody even manage to climb up to the window? This house is on twelve-foot-high stilts, and there's no deck outside the bedrooms."

"It looks like somebody got into the shed and grabbed the ladder I had stored there. They propped it against the house and climbed up."

Cassidy's grip on the girl's shoulder tightened.

An even more disturbing question circled in her mind. "How did someone even know she was here? And in that room?"

Ty's face tightened. "That's a great question."

Cassidy would ponder that later.

Right now, she wanted to get Janie cleaned up.

"WE NEED to go to the Blackout headquarters and stay there," Ty said. "I should have taken Janie there earlier, but I had no idea these people would be this bold."

Cassidy finished brushing Janie's freshly washed hair and nodded. "That sounds like a great idea. At least there's a security fence all around the facility."

"I'll get some of the guys to keep an eye on whichever building we stay in."

"I just can't get over the fact that someone tried to break into her room."

"I can't either," Ty said. "I'm liking this less and less all the time."

"I'll pack a few things so we can get ready to move over." She looked at the little girl. "Janie, why don't you grab the teddy bear and gather some of your pictures and crayons if you want to bring them."

Janie, eyes wide and frightened, moved quickly to gather her things.

Twenty minutes later, the three of them plus Kujo were in Ty's truck headed down the road.

Cassidy kept a lookout as they went, but she didn't see anything out of place. The black SUV seemed to be long gone.

Banks hadn't been able to locate that car. Cassidy had also asked Banks to come by the cottage to look for any evidence that may have been left behind. He got a cast of a footprint, but he didn't find any fingerprints on the shed's door handle or on the ladder.

Even the security cameras Ty had set up outside the place only picked up big shadows moving in the darkness. In other words, nothing that could help them.

Cassidy hoped that staying at Blackout would be a good choice. She knew they'd be safer there.

Previously, Blackout had been headquartered at Cassidy and Ty's cottage and the cabanas located behind it. But, as they'd grown, they'd needed a bigger facility.

Financial opportunities had allowed them to purchase a piece of property that had at one time been a campground. A cult had originally bought it before being forced off the island—and many of the members arrested.

Now, Blackout did all their trainings there. Over the past several months, multiple buildings had also been erected on the property, allowing for adequate housing and operational facilities, all within a fenced in area. The place was practically like a miniature military base.

The team had started with four guys, but four new recruits were coming in to start work soon. Cassidy had only met the new guys once, when they'd interviewed, but she knew if Ty and Colton had handpicked these guys, they were all outstanding.

Griff McIntyre met them at the gate and let them through before locking up behind them. They then pulled down a long lane until they reached a cluster of buildings that had recently been constructed.

The main building where the guys met for training and other meetings rose in the center of the property. Two wings branched from the middle of the facility, each containing various apartments. The other buildings around the facility were for people who came here for retreats or training.

The whole organization had really grown to be something much bigger than either Ty or Cassidy had expected, and God had opened many doors for that to happen.

At the main building, Cassidy and Ty unloaded the car before heading inside with Janie. They walked up the stairs to an apartment located near the center of the building. There were two bedrooms here, which would make the situation ideal.

Cassidy glanced beside her and saw that Janie's eyes were getting droopy.

She led her into the spare bedroom and tucked her in. "You're going to be safe here. I promise."

Cassidy knew that she would protect this girl with her life, as would Ty and his team of former SEALs.

But she had to wonder just how far these guys coming after Janie would go.

CHAPTER TWENTY

DOC CLEMSON WAS WAITING for Cassidy when she pulled into the police station the next morning.

She took another sip of the coffee she'd just picked up at The Crazy Chefette. How many of these cups would she need to make it through today? She knew she had a long day ahead of her and that she needed to be sharp.

She'd tried to sleep last night, but she had ended up tossing and turning. She knew they were safe at the compound. Benjamin James, one of the Blackout members, had been stationed outside to keep an eye on things.

Despite that, she felt restless. No area of her life felt safe—not with Janie being in danger and the person responsible acting so aggressively.

She paused near the front desk where Clemson entertained Paige with some kind of skeleton joke.

"Clemson . . . what brings you by?" Cassidy took another sip of her coffee.

Clemson sobered at the sight of her. "Cassidy Chambers . . . I had an update I wanted to tell you in person."

"Let's go to my office. Hopefully, it's good news." She led the way.

He lowered himself into the seat across from her and frowned. "I don't know if I would call it good news or not. But it's progress."

"I'll take progress. What's going on?" She set her coffee down on her desk and braced herself for whatever he was about to say.

"I got a call back from a firearms expert I contacted about the bodies found in the house next to the governor's rental," Clemson started. "Using the crime scene photos and results from my autopsy, he was able to determine the trajectory of the bullets."

"Okay . . ."

Clemson rubbed his jaw, almost as if he were hesitant to continue. "I know I initially said this was a murder-suicide. But then I had second thoughts about that. I'm glad I followed my hunch. Based on the trajectory of the bullets, there's no way that could be the case."

Cassidy sucked in a breath. She'd known this was a possibility but was still shocked. "What do you mean?"

"I mean, even if Larry shot his wife, just like we initially thought, there was no way Larry Taylor could have shot himself from the angle that he did."

"Different guns? Did they shoot each other at the same time?"

"The bullets matched. Same weapon."

"I looked into the gun we found. It was reported stolen from a place up in Hatteras three days ago. The police up there talked to the man it's registered to. He doesn't have a record and appears to be on the up and up."

"The suicide note threw us off, I'd say. But I thought it was strange that it wasn't signed."

"Speaking of which . . ." Cassidy glanced at her phone as a new message came in. "I have a sample of Larry's handwriting. His son sent it to me."

"And?" Clemson leaned closer.

"This is what it looks like." She held up her phone.

As Clemson took it from her, she pulled out a

photo of the suicide note and held it next to the sample she'd just been sent.

One thing was clear.

"There's no way Larry wrote this letter," Cassidy muttered.

"Someone forged it to throw us off track."

She leaned back as the harsh truth of the matter seemed to bolt itself to her until she could hardly breathe. "So the people who were staying in the house next to the governor were both murdered."

Clemson's gaze met hers. "That's right. I don't know what's going on here on this island, but it's not looking good."

CASSIDY SLIPPED on her jacket and started to the door after Clemson left.

She hadn't liked the news he'd told her. That, along with the man coming after Janie last night, confirmed something shady was going on here on Lantern Beach.

She'd bet anything that these incidents were somehow connected.

Before she stepped out from the police station, she nearly collided with someone coming inside.

Mac.

"Where's the fire?" He grabbed her arm as if concerned about her. It wasn't like Cassidy to be this distracted.

She released her breath, still trying to sort out her thoughts on everything that had happened. "No fire. I'm just on my way to see if I can talk to the governor."

He raised his eyebrows. "Dr. Wilbur I-Can't-Even-Say-Hi Hollick? Again? Everything okay?"

She shrugged. "I'm not sure. That's what I need to figure out."

"Want company?" He nodded toward her vehicle, looking nonchalant.

Cassidy knew him well enough to know he was chomping at the bit, so to speak, to dig into this investigation. "Why not?"

Mac fell into step beside her as she hurried to her SUV.

"What's going on?" Mac waited until they were inside her vehicle before asking the question. "Tell me more."

She filled him in on last night's events.

He let out a low whistle. "Things are getting hot here on Lantern Beach, and the summer scorch hasn't even started yet."

"You don't have to tell me." Cassidy shook her head at the thought of it.

"Do you think Governor Hollick is in some way tied with these incidents?"

"I don't know exactly what's going on. All I know is that apparently the same vehicle going past his house appeared also at my house last night. I need to figure out if that's a coincidence or not. I also need to know if there's any connection between this Larry and Linda Taylor and the governor."

"Things were boring around here until you arrived, Cassidy. You know that, don't you?"

She frowned. "Sometimes I wish they were boring again."

CHAPTER TWENTY-ONE

"ARE you trying to draw attention to our presence here?" Peter scowled at Cassidy as if she'd brought in the plague itself to the governor's rental.

"I have a few questions for Governor Hollick," she stated.

His cold stare burned into her. "I'm sorry. He's on vacation, and he's not meeting with anybody right now. It's something I like to refer to as 'time off.'"

Wasn't he a funny guy? If only bitterness didn't line his every word.

"I'm afraid this isn't about his job," Cassidy said. "It's about a situation here on the island."

A cool breeze swept through Peter's gaze. "Any meetings must be run through me."

Cassidy took a deep breath, trying to dispel her

anger. "If you must know, the car that you've seen driving past your house is now linked to another crime here on the island. We need to find out if the governor might know of some connection."

After a moment of silence, Peter finally nodded. "I see. Let me go speak with Governor Hollick, and I'll be back. Stay here." His tone was more of a command—and almost a put-down.

As soon as he turned his back on them, Cassidy turned to Mac and rolled her eyes.

She understood the role of security for a top government official needed to be taken seriously. But this guy . . . he was a piece of work.

"For the record, I didn't vote for Hollick," Mac added.

Cassidy fought a smile. "Good to know."

Just then, footsteps sounded down the hallway. Cassidy straightened when she saw the governor appear with Peter. The man was dressed more casually than Cassidy usually saw him in the news. He wore khaki shorts and a white shirt. Still, something about him seemed ready to throw on a tie and fake smile in case reporters came around with a press opportunity.

He nodded curtly to Mac and then Cassidy.

"Mayor. Chief. I hear you'd like a word with me about a local situation."

A local situation? Was that how Peter had described it?

Cassidy resisted another eye roll. "That's right. I'm sorry to stop by unannounced. Is there somewhere we might be able to talk in private?"

He pointed to a room beside them—a smaller, more intimate conversation area than the large rooms in the rest of the house. "Let's go in here. My wife and son are outside at the pool—it's heated this time of year. We have the house to ourselves right now."

After they were all seated, Cassidy pulled out her phone. "As you may have heard, a little girl was found washed up on the beach here this week."

"Someone mentioned that to me," Hollick said. "That's just terrible. Have you had any luck locating her parents yet?"

"Unfortunately, we haven't," Cassidy said. "That's why we're here."

"Do you think *I* know her parents?" He raised his eyebrows as if the idea was incredulous.

"Not necessarily. But we suspect the same car that's been driving past your house was seen last night outside my own home after an abduction attempt on the little girl."

His eyebrows climbed higher. "I can't imagine what this has to do with me. The past few months have been turbulent, but no one knows I'm here."

He glanced at Peter as if confirming the notion.

Peter nodded reassuringly.

"We're trying to find the link here," Cassidy continued. "We're trying to turn every stone in hopes of finding answers."

"Of course. I'll do anything you need."

Cassidy resisted the urge to flash a satisfied smile at Peter. There was nothing humorous about this situation. But his need for control seemed to permeate the air around them, and it felt good to see him overturned.

"Great." Cassidy found Janie's photo on her phone and showed it to Governor Hollick. "Have you ever seen this girl before?"

He took the phone from her and studied the picture before shaking his head. "I'm sorry. But she doesn't look familiar."

"She's not the daughter of one of your friends or staff members?"

"Not that I'm aware of." He glanced at Peter. "Have you ever seen her before?"

Peter's icy gaze went to the phone, and he shook his head. "No, I haven't."

"Have you received any specific threats lately?" Cassidy continued.

The governor glanced at Peter again before shaking his head. "Threats are generally just a part of this job. So, yes, I have received threats. I'm not sure which ones are credible, however."

Cassidy turned to Peter. "Do you have any more insight on this?"

"There are no known active threats at this moment."

Something about the way he said the words made Cassidy wonder if there was something he wasn't saying.

"I see," Cassidy said. "If either of you think of anything, I'd appreciate you letting me know."

"Of course." Governor Hollick shifted, as if ready to stand and wrap this up. "Is there anything else I can help you with in the meantime?"

"There's just one more thing that I wanted to mention." Cassidy hesitated to share this next bit of news. "We discovered that the two people who were staying in the cottage next door . . . their deaths weren't a murder-suicide. They were both murdered."

The governor gasped. "And I thought this place was safe."

"I assure you that we're trying to get to the bottom of whatever is going on here." She found a picture of the couple and showed it to the governor. "Do you recognize this couple? The Taylors?"

He looked at the photo before handing the phone back to Cassidy. "I've never seen them before. I wish I could help. I really do. But I'm unsure if this has anything to do with me at all. Really, all I want is to enjoy some downtime with my family. I work twelve-hour days most of the year, even more than that sometimes with the new legislation that we've passed. I'd really like some quiet time if you don't mind."

"I understand." Cassidy gave him a polite nod. "I appreciate your time."

Peter stepped forward. "Let me escort you two to the door."

Without wasting any more time, Cassidy and Mac were led outside.

But Cassidy's mind still remained on the conversation inside.

AS SOON AS Mac and Cassidy climbed back into Cassidy's SUV, Mac turned to her. "What did you think of that?"

Cassidy frowned, in no hurry to head down the road, she paused. "I felt like the two of them should have tried harder to assist us. I want to respect the governor's boundaries, and I realize he's on vacation. But he seemed rather anxious for us to leave. I don't think all this is a coincidence. I need to find the connection."

"That's going to be hard to do without Governor Hollick's cooperation."

Her frown deepened, and she pulled the visor down to keep the sun from her eyes. "That's what I'm afraid of also. In my mind, the only reason he *wouldn't* cooperate is because he knows something that would make him look bad."

"There are a lot of rumors about some deals he's done. He was a physician before he was the governor, and his family were businesspeople. He handed over control of the corporations he inherited to other family members once he was elected."

Cassidy didn't like the sound of that. Then again, she hadn't met too many upstanding politicians—other than Mac, of course. "So maybe this isn't even related to the fact he's governor? Maybe this is somehow connected with something that a member of his family has done."

"It's definitely a possibility worth exploring." Mac sighed before glancing at her. "What are you going to do now?"

"I'm going to head back to the station and continue to look into Larry and Linda Taylor's backgrounds. The answers are out there. I just need to figure out what the connection points are between these cases."

"If you need my assistance, you know I'm here for you."

As tempting as that sounded . . . "Helping me any further in this investigation might put you on the governor's bad side."

"That's a risk I am willing to take."

Cassidy glanced at him, hoping that the gratitude showed in her eyes. "Thank you, Mac. I can't tell you how much that means to me."

He winked. "Anytime, kiddo. Anytime."

CHAPTER TWENTY-TWO

CASSIDY SPENT the next three hours back in her office examining every aspect of Larry and Linda Taylor's lives. She still had no answers.

Everything about the couple seemed squeaky clean. She had no idea why someone would want them dead.

Unless it was a crime of opportunity.

What if Larry and Linda just happened to be in the wrong place at the wrong time?

What if that other couple, the Ballards, had ended up renting that house? Would they be the ones who were dead now?

It was a possibility worth exploring.

What about Peter, the governor's head of security? He was an edgy guy.

Cassidy had been around a lot of bodyguards and security-type men and women. She knew what they were like and could respect their sometimes not-so-sunny dispositions.

But Peter's attitude went beyond that. He was borderline hostile.

Was he protecting Governor Hollick for some other reason? Did his loyalty run deeper than a mere professional service?

Questions turned over in Cassidy's mind again and again. But nothing made sense. Not yet at least.

Finally, at lunchtime, she decided she needed to step away from the investigation for a minute.

Ty called and asked if they could meet at The Crazy Chefette. His friends were keeping an eye on Janie, and he needed to run to the store to pick up a few things anyway. Cassidy knew she could trust the Blackout gang to watch the girl.

Besides, she and Ty could use a minute to talk alone.

Whenever they'd been at the house, Janie was always close, and there were some things they just couldn't say in front of the girl.

As soon as Cassidy walked into The Crazy Chefette and the scent of fried seafood and spicy seasoning surrounded her, she instantly felt better.

This restaurant—though it was nothing fancy—almost felt like a second home to her.

Ty sat at their normal booth—one in the corner where they could both keep an eye on the place, as was instinct for law enforcement and security personnel.

Austin and Wes, two of their good friends, stood nearby talking to Ty. As soon as Cassidy walked over, Lisa emerged from the back with her baby in her arms.

Cassidy's heart practically melted at the sight of her.

"If it isn't my little Julia." Cassidy's voice instantly went from tough police chief to jelly-spined baby lover. "How are you doing today, little angel?"

The girl offered a toothless grin as she looked at Cassidy and reached for her face. Cassidy made duck lips and tickled the girl's belly for a minute. "You are getting *so* big."

The baby grinned even wider in return. She really was adorable. So, so adorable.

Another pang of longing rushed through Cassidy, but she ignored it.

Lisa turned her attention from Julia to Cassidy. "Good to see you in here. I know this new case is keeping you busy. I was getting worried that you weren't eating."

Now that she mentioned it, Cassidy's clothes were feeling a bit looser lately. Not just because of this case. Her weight loss had started a month or two ago when she realized that her dreams of having a baby might not ever happen.

That's what the doctor had told her, at least.

"Don't you worry about me." Cassidy patted her ever-flattening stomach. "I'll be just fine."

Lisa's eyebrows flickered up, as if she doubted Cassidy's words. Then a smile returned to her face. "I'm going to bring you out something to eat. No arguments. This one is on me."

Cassidy smiled before sliding into the booth across from Ty and chitchatting with the guys for a minute.

Austin and Wes stayed, catching up for a few more minutes until Lisa delivered Cassidy a plate full of crunchy fried chicken strips, jalapeño-infused waffles, and cherry-flavored syrup—one of her unique creations.

The meal smelled divine.

Ty's food came out at the same time—a jalapeño popper bacon burger and fries. Cassidy glanced through the little window into the kitchen and saw

Skye there, bouncing Julia in her arms. She must be helping Lisa out today since Braden was working.

Austin and Wes went back to their own table, and Ty and Cassidy turned to each other. They had a lot to talk about. Cassidy wished things didn't feel so tense between them lately. But the stress of unsuccessfully trying to have a child for the past year had taken its toll on them.

"How's Janie?" Cassidy stared at Ty from across the table.

Janie's safety was the most important thing. This wasn't the time to think about her own losses or grief. She had a job to do—a job she cared deeply about.

She was personally responsible for keeping Janie unharmed.

"She really loves Ada," Ty said. "The two have been playing all day."

That was something to be thankful for, at least. "Has Janie said anything yet?"

Ty shook his head. "No, not yet. But she *did* smile a couple of times. Maybe she's slowly breaking out of her shell."

"This morning, I put in a call to a child psychologist who works for the county. The earliest she can get out here is in three days."

"Too bad Elise is up at the conference near DC for a few days," Ty said.

Elise was Colton's wife, and one of the best psychologists around—not to mention an all-around fantastic person. She was presenting several lectures at the Association for Cognitive Behaviors Symposium.

"I know. I thought about Elise also." Cassidy took a bite of her chicken and let the flavors wash over her tastebuds. Lisa never disappointed. The combination of maple syrup, savory chicken, and jalapeños was spot on.

"The Donovans, even though we don't know their real identities, said their 'daughter' was mildly autistic. At first, I wondered if that was an excuse they thought up in advance of picking her up—just in case she panicked. But what if Janie really is on the spectrum? Could that be another reason why she's not speaking?"

Ty shrugged, his gaze making it clear he was unconvinced. "I suppose that would be a possibility, but I haven't noticed any other indicators that would lead me to believe she has special needs. But it's really hard to say, especially given the trauma that she's been through."

Cassidy nodded. "I agree. You guys haven't seen

anything suspicious over at the Blackout compound, right?"

"It's been peaceful today. Believe me, all the guys have been on guard and are taking shifts watching the grounds." Ty picked up a french fry and took a bite.

His heathered blue T-shirt showed off his strong physique—but not in a narcissistic, look-at-me type of way. He was strong, but nothing about his strength was for show. He was strong because that was what was required of him—first, as a SEAL. Now, as a husband and leader.

It was one more thing Cassidy admired about him.

"I appreciate that, especially since I know that you guys have other things going on," Cassidy said.

"It's no problem. Really, it's not." He picked up another fry and dipped it into the vat of ketchup he'd poured onto his plate. He had very few flaws, but his love of ketchup was one of them. "So what's going on with you? Any updates that you can tell me about?"

"I wish I had something. But every time I think I have a lead, I come to a dead end." Cassidy filled him in on her day, including her visit with the governor and the research she'd done into the Ballards and Taylors.

One side of Ty's face twitched the same way it always did when he wasn't happy about something. "I don't like the idea that the governor might be hiding something."

"I don't like it either. But Janie isn't talking, the couple who died in the house beside the governor's obviously can't tell us anything, and the governor claims ignorance. He's not willing to share any information. Or, to give him the benefit of the doubt, maybe he truly doesn't know anything."

"Maybe." Ty frowned.

Cassidy could tell he didn't agree with that benefit-of-the-doubt assessment. But they had no evidence to say otherwise.

"What's your next step?" Ty asked.

Cassidy pressed her lips together in thought before frowning. "That's exactly what I need to figure out."

OFFICER BANKS CALLED Cassidy and told her he'd been able to locate the Ballards—the couple who'd double-booked at the house beside the governor. Cassidy said she wanted to talk to them herself, and Ty volunteered to go with her.

He'd feel better if someone had her back, especially considering everything going on lately.

It wasn't only that worrying Ty, however.

He'd noticed a vague emptiness in Cassidy lately, and he knew that it was wearing on her that they may never be able to have kids of their own.

He wished that he could take away some of the hurt, that he could change things. But some things were just in God's hands, and they had to trust that all the details would work out despite any heartache they felt.

Plus, Ty wasn't giving up hope yet.

He hoped Cassidy's tests would come back positive and that the doctor could offer some kind of solution.

"What do you know about these people?" Ty asked as they headed down the road, Cassidy behind the wheel.

"Apparently, Ed and Sandra are in their thirties. They don't have any kids. They came here from upstate New York, and they both love kiteboarding."

"So where have they been the past couple of days as you guys have been trying to get in touch with them?"

Cassidy's jaw tightened. "That's one of the first questions I plan on asking them."

Ty settled back in his seat as they continued down the road.

Did this couple have anything to do with what was going on?

Ty knew that Cassidy was smart to check them out.

In his days as a Navy SEAL, he'd tracked down some of the world's most hardened criminals. He's been on the front lines of danger more times than he could count.

But nothing felt scarier than having a loved one in danger.

Sometimes, that made Lantern Beach feel entirely more dangerous than the Middle East had.

Cassidy was good at her job. She was well equipped to do what she needed to do. And she was smart.

But as a SEAL, Ty had always worked with a team. There was a reason for that. As the old saying went, there truly was safety in numbers.

That's why Ty was glad he could go with Cassidy now. He trusted that Janie was in good hands with his guys. Besides, as much as he hadn't minded keeping an eye on her, it felt good to get out and do some hands-on work himself.

They pulled up to an oceanfront house probably five blocks from where the governor was currently staying.

After parking the car, Ty followed Cassidy toward the front door. Another car had been parked in the driveway—a car with New York plates—so it looked like this couple should be home.

Cassidy strode up the steps to the front door and rang the bell. As she did, Ty remained behind her, a quiet but protective presence.

A moment later, a man opened the door.

And he had a gun in his hand.

CHAPTER TWENTY-THREE

CASSIDY REACHED for her weapon as soon as she spotted the Glock in the man's hand.

Before she could tell him to freeze, his eyes widened. He lowered his weapon and stepped back.

"You're a cop. I'm sorry." The man set his gun on a table and raised his hands. "I wasn't sure who was here."

The man was clearly Ed Ballard. Cassidy had seen his picture earlier.

Cassidy narrowed her gaze. "Are you expecting someone else?"

The man's shoulders slumped. "No, but I heard what happened to that other couple. I have been on edge ever since."

"I'm Police Chief Cassidy Chambers, and this is

my husband, Ty. Do you mind if we come in to talk to you?"

"No. Of course not." Ed stepped aside to allow them to come in.

Cassidy kept her eye on that man's gun as she did so. She could never be too careful or too trusting in a situation like this.

He nodded toward the living room beside him, and the three of them sat down on a pastel-colored sectional. A gigantic picture window displayed the ocean outside, and the scent of fried seafood seemed to float in the air.

A moment later, a woman who introduced herself as Sandra, his wife, came and sat beside them.

"We've been looking for you," Cassidy started.

The Ballards glanced at each other before Sandra finally spoke.

"We heard what happened at that other house, and we got spooked." Sandra frowned, almost looking apologetic or sheepish. "Ed and I had been talking about an overnight trip to Ocracoke, just to experience something different. After everything that happened, we decided there was no better time."

"Did you take the ferry?" Cassidy asked.

"No, we hired a private charter, just to keep things on the down low," Ed said.

"I need the name and number of whatever captain you used," Cassidy said.

"Of course," Ed said. "We used Jack Darrow. He seems like a fixture around here."

"He is." Cassidy didn't miss a beat. "Why were you spooked?"

"We were supposed to stay in that house," Ed said. "What if we were the ones who were supposed to be killed?"

"You sound awfully convinced that this was murder. Why is that?" Cassidy hadn't released that information to the public yet.

Ed frowned. "Those people . . . they didn't know anybody in the area. They were thrilled to come here but disheartened about the beach house. Sure, all of us exchanged words with each other. After all, Sandra and I arrived at the same time they did. We all assumed we'd start a nice, relaxing vacation. It was clear that only one of us could win."

"And the other couple won?"

Ed shrugged. "I suppose I saw it that way at first. But I didn't really hold it against them. After all, they did officially have their reservation in first."

"And you guys were able to find this place?"

Cassidy glanced at the high ceiling and great view. "Not a bad trade-off."

"That's right," Ed said. "We were upset, so we didn't use the same management company. We didn't want to reward them with any more of our business, so we found another vacation rental company and they set us up here. In the end, I can't help but think that we got the better house."

"What surprises me is how convinced you are that this was a murder and that it could have been you." Cassidy watched their expressions carefully. What weren't they telling her?

"We just assumed this couple was robbed and shot in the process," Ed said. "That's what makes sense to me. I think if we had been there, it would have been us."

Yet the two of them had been so spooked, they'd left the island for a night to hide out, almost like they feared somebody might track them down. That's what didn't make sense to Cassidy.

"I know what you're thinking," Sandra rushed, almost looking desperate to convince Cassidy of their story. "I know all this sounds weird. But Ed and I didn't know what was going on."

"Yet you came back . . ." Cassidy said.

"After some time away from this area, things

started to make more sense," Ed said. "We realized that we probably weren't in danger, and that this other couple was probably in the wrong place at the wrong time. We overreacted."

Cassidy shifted, still holding her notepad and pen so she could scribble notes. "Did this other couple say anything interesting? According to what you've told me, they seemed pretty happy to be here and like they knew no one else."

Sandra nodded. "That's correct. The man said that business has been stressful lately, and they were happy to be able to get away for a while. They also said it was the first time they'd left their bakery since they opened it, and they were a little bit nervous about leaving somebody else in charge."

"Is there anything else you can think of that might be significant for this case? Anything these two said or did or brought with them?"

The two of them glanced at each other again before shaking their heads.

"No," Ed said. "I'm sorry. But there's not."

Cassidy pulled out her card and placed it on the table. "If you think of anything else, let me know. How long do you plan on being here in town?"

"Until the end of the week," Sandra said.

"Although we are tempted to leave earlier. It's hard to relax when you keep thinking about murder."

Cassidy wanted to argue with her, but she couldn't.

Because Sandra's words made perfect sense.

"DO you think those two are innocent?" Ty asked as soon as he and Cassidy climbed back into Cassidy's SUV.

"I have a feeling they're hiding something." Cassidy stared out the windshield and shook her head. "But I'm not sure what that would be. Their reactions simply don't match the events that took place. Why go hide when there's been no threat against you?"

"I agree," Ty said. "However, their actions don't mean they're killers either."

"Agreed. But I am going to continue to look into them. I'm going to follow up with the captain and see if he has anything to say."

"Smart idea."

Cassidy glanced over at him and let out a breath, not bothering to take the SUV out of Park . "Do you want to go with me or do you want to go back?"

"As much as I love being with you, I should probably get back now."

"I can't blame you," Cassidy said. "I'll drop you off at your truck and try to come by for dinner later. I want to see you and Janie, to see how she's doing."

"That sounds great."

A few minutes later, they pulled up to The Crazy Chefette. Ty kissed her cheek and then climbed out to get into his truck.

Cassidy pulled away and headed toward the harbor so she could talk to Captain Jack Darrow and confirm the Ballards' alibi.

That wasn't the man's real name, just the moniker he used to drum up business here on the island, and it seemed to work well for him.

Cassidy hoped that Captain Darrow might have some answers for her.

CHAPTER TWENTY-FOUR

CAPTAIN JACK HAD PROVEN UNHELPFUL. Cassidy had caught him at the docks, which had felt fortuitous since he spent most of his days out on the water. The waves were a little too choppy today to go out, he'd told her.

He had said that Ed and Sandra seemed to be a little jumpy on their charter. They'd whispered a lot. But their financials checked out, and they were indeed with Darrow the whole time.

Cassidy tucked that information away in the back of her mind as she headed to the station. She had several things that she still needed to look into.

First, she needed to follow up with the Coast Guard to see if they had heard anything else about any potential shipwrecks within the past week.

Cassidy had expected more things to wash ashore if that had been the case.

But nothing else had turned up on the beach recently.

She also wanted to look into some of the governor's family businesses.

Maybe it was nothing. But, on the other hand, maybe that detail could be everything. She didn't want to leave any stone unturned, as the saying went.

But after two more hours of working at the station, Cassidy hadn't discovered anything new.

The Coast Guard had no new information. They agreed with her assessment that there didn't seem to be a shipwreck involved here.

That brought Cassidy back to the question of what happened to the girl. Why had she been in those angry ocean waters wearing a life jacket?

It just didn't make sense if it was anything other than a shipwreck.

And that bothered her. It bothered her *a lot*.

As did the fact that there had been a double murder on the island.

Her officers had been busy looking for witnesses.

But, because of the secluded location of the

home, there hadn't been anyone around. Nor had there been any security cameras nearby.

One thing Clemson had told her stuck in her mind.

Based on the clean angle of the shots, it almost seemed like the work of a professional.

If that was true, why would a professional killer target the owners of a bakery?

Her team would continue to work the case until they found answers. But Cassidy still held the belief that all these cases might somehow be connected.

As Cassidy sat at her desk, she stared at the picture of Janie. She'd taken one—with the girl's permission—last night.

In the photo, Janie sat on the couch, that teddy bear in her lap, and stared with a blank look at the camera.

Cassidy had printed it at work this morning. Now, every time she felt like giving up, she looked at that photo and knew she had to fight for this girl.

She had been in this profession long enough to know that most of the time answers didn't simply drop into your lap. She had to dig and then dig some more. Sometimes, she'd realize while digging that she was in a totally wrong area. Sometimes, she had to move to a new location, one with more roots and even more obstacles. That process seemed to repeat itself several times.

But eventually, answers could generally be found. The occasional cold case popped up, but Cassidy prayed that wasn't the situation right now.

Dillinger knocked on her door before stepping inside. Based on the hooded look to his eyes, he had something on his mind.

"What's going on?"

"This may be nothing," he started. "But I want to mention it, just in case. I've been reviewing all the evidence, and something about those alcohol swabs made me want to look into them a little bit more."

"Okay . . ."

"Anyway, it turns out they were made by a company called Buxton Pharmaceuticals."

Cassidy wasn't sure where he was going with this, but she couldn't wait to hear.

"At first, I didn't think there would be any connection between a pharmaceutical company and what was going on here on Lantern Beach. But I dug a little bit deeper. It turns out that Buxton Pharmaceuticals filed a lawsuit against Governor Hollick."

Cassidy's back straightened. "Really?"

"I'm trying to find out more details now."

Her pulse raced. It looked like they finally had another lead. That was an answer to prayer.

"Send me anything that you have on this, and let's keep digging," Cassidy said.

"Will do."

As he turned to leave, Cassidy called to him. "Good job, Dillinger."

"Thanks, Chief."

WHAT DILLINGER HAD TOLD Cassidy was correct. Governor Hollick was in the middle of a lawsuit with the CEO of Buxton Pharmaceuticals.

The National Institutes of Health had pulled funding for a new drug the company had been researching for five years. From what Cassidy could tell, the medication was supposed to cure ALS, also known as Lou Gehrig's disease.

But certainly the governor wasn't responsible for where funding went through NIH, so why was he being personally sued?

Cassidy did more online research before leaning back in her chair.

Hollick had been a doctor before he became governor, and he'd worked for the NIH for two years.

The president of Buxton Pharm must hold him personally responsible for some reason.

As far as Cassidy could tell, that new medication had never been released.

Had the project been shelved because of funding?

How did this fit? That was the question.

She could go ask the governor, and she probably would.

But he most likely would tell her that he didn't know anything.

She tapped her chin as her thoughts continued to turn over.

On a whim, she picked up the phone and dialed the number for Buxton Pharmaceuticals. A receptionist answered, Cassidy explained to her who she was, and then she asked to speak with the CEO, someone named Richard Robertson.

As she waited on hold, she pulled up information on the company online. They'd developed several drugs that she'd heard about before. Their website was crisp and professional.

She clicked on a tab with information about Robertson and studied his picture.

The man was probably in his early fifties. His face was so thin that his bones protruded at his cheeks and around his eyes. His black-and-white hair was cut neatly.

"Richard Robertson."

A voice came on the line, jostling Cassidy from the computer screen.

He'd actually picked up.

She cleared her throat before explaining who she was.

"What can I do for you?" Robertson's voice sounded crisp and his words fast.

Cassidy explained she was calling in regard to an investigation before launching into her questions. "A bag full of your alcohol swabs recently washed up here on the island."

"I'm not sure what that has to do with me," he said. "Hospitals and doctors' offices, among other places, often buy our supplies in bulk."

"I realize that, and I realize that I might be reaching here. But if you'll bear with me, I have a few questions I'd like to ask you."

"Of course. What are your questions pertaining to?"

"They're pertaining to the lawsuit you filed against North Carolina's Governor Wilbur Hollick a couple of months ago."

A pause stretched between them. "Oh, that. The

executives and I aren't huge fans of the governor, by any means. When he worked for the NIH, he personally made it a point to pull funding on an important project we'd been working on for years. My team was on the edge of discovering a breakthrough medication when Hollick decided that we couldn't get any more money."

"Why did he do that?"

Robertson let out a sigh. "His public answer was that there was no more funding to be given and that we'd been given enough already. But everybody on the inside knew it was because Hollick wanted to give that very funding to his brother's company, most likely so he could get a kickback."

Cassidy frowned. "That sounds illegal."

"It is. But it's also unprovable."

Cassidy jotted a few notes as they spoke. "What happened with this breakthrough medication since then?"

"Hollick's decision put us about a year behind. Eventually, we did find a new investor, and now we're back on track."

"At least that's good news."

"Pardon me for being blunt, but I'm still not sure why you're calling me."

Cassidy drew in a deep breath as she contemplated how much to say. "We've had several suspicious events happen here on our island, and I'm just trying to follow every lead. I really appreciate your help in this matter."

"If you're calling because you think the governor might be up to something, I'd encourage you to trust your gut. That man is a snake. I wouldn't put anything past him. And I'm telling you that as someone who has dealt with him personally on more than one occasion."

The man's words left no room for argument.

Cassidy ended the call and leaned back at her desk, her thoughts turning over and over again.

Just where were the puzzle pieces going to lead her?

That was the question.

CHAPTER TWENTY-FIVE

CASSIDY HAD to be careful how she played her cards, so to speak. She wanted to talk to the governor again. But if she approached him once more, she might use all the goodwill the man had toward her on the visit. She needed to make sure there was nothing else she needed to ask him about before she spent what might be her last opportunity.

Instead, just as she had promised, she left at dinnertime and went to the Blackout compound. She called hello to several people before she made her way up to the apartment where she, Ty, and Janie were staying.

As soon as she walked in, she noticed that Janie wasn't there.

Ty stood from his computer and greeted her.

"She's still playing with Ada. The two are getting along fabulously."

"That's good news, at least."

"And don't worry. Griff is in there with them."

"I'm not worried, not about that anyway." Cassidy sat on the couch, tugging Ty down beside her. She trusted Ty and knew that he made wise choices.

"What's new?" Ty asked.

She filled him in on everything that had happened.

Ty leaned back, as if her update had been heavier than he'd expected. "So we have a mute girl we found on the beach. We have alcohol swabs from a company that's had direct conflict with the governor, who just happens to be staying on the island. And the murdered couple was staying in the house beside the governor's rental. The question is, how do all these things fit?"

"That's what I am trying to figure out also. It looks like I can clear Ed and Sandra and take them off my suspect list. So who does that leave?"

"What about the governor?" Ty asked.

Cassidy's eyebrows shot up. "If we're talking about the couple who was murdered, Governor

Hollick definitely wasn't on the island when that happened."

Ty shrugged. "He could have paid somebody to do his dirty work. Someone like his head of security."

"I agree. He *could* have done that. But I'm not sure I think that's what happened."

"Do you still think that Janie's parents are somehow involved in all this?"

"I'm not sure." Cassidy frowned and tucked her legs beneath her. "I don't want to read more into things than I should. But I don't want to ignore what could seem like a coincidence either."

He leaned forward and squeezed her hand. "I have total confidence in your abilities. You're going to figure this out."

She smiled, appreciating the reassurance.

But right now, she wanted to see Janie, wanted to see for herself that the girl was okay.

"One more thing," Ty said. "Gail called and said she'd like to stop by for a visit in two days. I didn't tell her we were staying here because I didn't know how it would go over."

Cassidy's stomach clenched.

One more obstacle she needed to deal with.

Would Gail try to take Janie away when she

learned about everything that had happened?

Cassidy couldn't say for sure.

But she needed to do everything in her power to make sure that this girl remained safe.

CASSIDY KNOCKED ON THE DOOR, and Griff answered. The man—though edgy at times—became a teddy bear around his daughter.

"These two are having a great time," he murmured.

"Any chance Janie has spoken to Ada?" Cassidy whispered.

Griff shook his head. "No, I'm sorry." He stepped aside, and Cassidy spotted Janie and Ada playing together on the floor. She smiled at the sight of it.

If she didn't know any better, she might have thought that Janie was just an ordinary little girl having fun with a friend. She might not have guessed all the trauma the girl had been through.

Janie's eyes lit when she saw Cassidy, and the girl sprang to her feet. She rushed toward Cassidy and threw her arms around her.

Warmth filled Cassidy. "Hey, sweetie. It looks like you're having fun."

"We . . . have . . . fun!" From her position on the rug, Ada annunciated each syllable like only a four-year-old could.

"Are you ready to get something to eat?" Cassidy asked Janie.

Janie didn't say anything, but Cassidy knew by the look in her eyes that she was.

With an arm around her shoulders, she told Griff thank you before heading back to her apartment.

Ty had fixed some baked chicken with potatoes and a salad. Everything was set up on the table when Cassidy and Janie got back.

Dinner felt surprisingly normal. Even though Janie didn't speak, Cassidy and Ty chitchatted as if she were a part of the conversation. Cassidy knew that the girl was listening. She could see it in her eyes.

After they finished eating and as Ty began to clean up, Cassidy pulled out some paper and crayons. She set them on the kitchen table in front of Janie.

Cassidy leaned toward the girl. "You did such a good job with your other drawings. Could you draw me another picture now?"

Janie glanced at her with those wide eyes before looking at the paper and picking up a crayon.

She began to sketch something on the white sheet of paper.

As she did, Cassidy helped Ty clean up.

Several minutes later, Cassidy walked over to Janie to look at the picture the girl had drawn.

Cassidy's breath caught when she saw the images there.

It was a picture of a boat. On one side of the vessel were two stick figures—one who appeared to be a man and the other a woman.

And on the other side was another man, one who held a knife in his hands.

As Cassidy sucked in a quick breath, Ty came to stand beside her. He dried his hands on a dishtowel as he peered over her shoulder.

Another glance at the picture revealed something that Cassidy had originally assumed was a wave.

But it wasn't.

It was a person in the water.

A person with a smaller head and body than the rest of the stick figures.

Almost like a child.

Cassidy's heart leapt into her throat.

Was Janie trying to tell them what had happened to her?

CHAPTER TWENTY-SIX

THE NEXT MORNING, Cassidy swung by to chat with Mac in his office. As she'd been sleeping, an idea had come to her. She felt confident that it was what she needed to do.

But she wanted Mac's advice first.

She knocked on the door before stepping inside. Today, Mac was playing *Call of Duty* on a computer he had tucked away in the corner.

She was sure he considered this research or a way to remain fluid with his shooting skills.

But his VR headset when combined with his ninja-like moves made Cassidy smile.

He quickly pulled them off and offered a sheepish grin.

He placed his headset on his desk and straightened. “Cassidy . . . what brings you by?”

“I need your feedback and wisdom.” She sat down in the chair across from him.

“Of course. What’s going on?” He lowered himself into his seat, his elbows on his desk, as he listened.

Cassidy swallowed hard before starting. She hoped she didn’t sound crazy. “When we first found Janie, I didn’t want many people to know about her presence here on the island so I could protect her.”

“That makes sense, especially considering what happened.”

“But now I realize that the people who are after her already know she’s here.”

Mac tilted his head to the side and nodded. “Another good point.”

“So what I’m wondering is this: I’d like to put out a press release stating that the police need help with identifying a child found on the beach.”

“I thought you wanted to keep everything under wraps.”

“I did—and part of me still does. But I’m wondering if putting the information out there could bring about somebody who could identify her.

And maybe if we can identify her, we can find out more answers."

"Yet, if this girl was from a loving home, you'd think we would have already heard something about her disappearance," Mac said.

"I've thought of that also. But maybe this new move will lead to some of those answers we so desperately need."

Mac remained quiet for a moment, staring at Cassidy. She could see the thoughts turning in his mind.

Finally, after a moment, he nodded. "I think it's a good idea. Make these guys play on your terms. Because you're right—whoever is behind this already knows that Janie is here. There's no need to keep it a secret any longer."

Good. He agreed.

Mac leaned back, his expression turning stonier. "You do realize that you are going to need to field a lot more phone calls if you do this. It's going to take up a tremendous amount of your time."

"I know." Cassidy frowned. "I thought of that too, and I hate to waste too much of my time fielding leads that go nowhere."

"That's definitely going to happen. People trying

to be helpful will call and offer information, but it will be nothing."

Cassidy mulled over that a moment, trying to figure out a good solution. "I'm sure I can get Paige and maybe one of my other officers to take the lead on answering the phone on those calls."

Mac's gaze locked with hers. "Why don't you let me help out?"

Cassidy stiffened, unsure if she'd heard him correctly. "You wouldn't mind? I know you're busy running the town and everything."

He twisted his lips and neck at the same time. "You'd be surprised at how un-busy this job is. Mind-numbingly so. I wouldn't mind helping at all. In fact, I'd be honored."

"That would be a huge help." Cassidy knew she could trust Mac's judgment.

His expression turned more serious. "Besides, depending on how this goes, someone might need to act as spokesman. It's better me than you."

His words washed over her. Mac was right.

Cassidy couldn't risk having her face on national TV. Not even regional TV.

If the wrong people found out she was still alive . . . her life here would be over.

"You're right," Cassidy said. "You should take the lead."

Despite Mac's reassurance that she was doing the right thing, her lungs still felt tight.

This could go incredibly right.

Or so incredibly wrong.

TWO HOURS LATER, everything was set in motion.

Janie's picture had been distributed to news outlets within a two-hour vicinity of Lantern Beach. A hotline had been set up. And Mac had taken the lead on it. Anybody who called with information would be directed to him.

Nobody would need to know Cassidy's name even.

Cassidy stood from her desk and stretched her legs. She'd been sitting for entirely too long. She didn't have much time, so she settled on pacing her office area as she took a quick break.

She was so thankful that Mac was here to help her.

She also knew that Blackout members would help if Cassidy said the word.

It wasn't so much that she thought she might need their help fielding calls. But she'd definitely need their help in watching over Janie, especially depending on what these events brought forth.

She glanced at her watch. The first news stories would probably begin popping up online within the hour. That was when the twelve o'clock news aired.

That meant she had another hour of relative calm before the storm started.

She prayed she'd done the right thing—for Janie's sake.

She kept thinking about that picture that Janie had drawn. The one with the boat. With a man with a knife. With the child in the water.

In her mind, she pictured Janie out to sea with her mother and father. Had they been coerced onto the vessel? It was a possibility.

Had someone—the man with the knife—pushed Janie into the water?

But what about the life jacket? If someone had tossed Janie in the water, why put a life vest on her? Why write Cassidy's name on that same flotation device?

Had someone been trying to toy with Cassidy?

It was a distinct possibility. She couldn't rule anything out.

But why Cassidy?

So much didn't make sense.

She broke away from her thoughts as Banks stepped into her office with a paper in hand. "I have an update that you're going to want to hear."

Cassidy sank back into her seat and braced herself for whatever new news she might be about to learn.

CHAPTER TWENTY-SEVEN

"I FINALLY GOT a hit on the couple who came in here claiming to be our Jane Doe's parents," Banks said.

Cassidy sat up straighter, all her attention suddenly on him. "What did you find out?"

"The two of them are actually criminals for hire. Their real names are Lars and Emma Shackleford. They're married and are former CIA officers who went rogue and started their own business with an emphasis on anything illegal."

Cassidy sucked in a breath. "That sounds serious."

Banks nodded, his expression stony. "Very serious. They're wanted for four counts of murder, among other things."

She wasn't feeling any better yet. "Tell me more."

"They appear to be based primarily out of the Baltimore area, although they work internationally." Banks laid some papers on her desk. "Feel free to look through all the reports I have on them. It will take a while. But they're wanted by several different law enforcement agencies."

Cassidy shuffled through a few of the police reports. These people were suspected in the shooting of a former DOD employee near DC, for the murder of two former SEALs in California, and for potentially poisoning a political candidate in Wisconsin.

These people weren't *just* criminals.

They were hardcore, no-holds-barred criminals.

Something else struck her. Clemson had said that the Taylors' deaths looked almost like a professional had done it.

Could the Shacklefords have killed them? Had their deaths been a hit?

Who would hire these guys? It had to be someone with money and power.

Even as Cassidy asked herself the question, only one person came to mind.

Governor Hollick.

He had the connections *and* the resources to do so.

But why in the world would the governor want to kill the Taylors?

Was this about Janie? That was what didn't make sense.

Could Janie be his illegitimate child?

Was someone threatening to go public with that information unless he did something?

The questions turned over in her head.

Cassidy glanced up at Banks after her quick perusal. "When were they last seen? What's the most updated status on them?"

"Nothing since they were here. They obviously got away, and they obviously know what they are doing."

Cassidy frowned as she glanced at those articles again. "Whoever is behind this is taking it very seriously. No expense has been spared."

Banks frowned. "I was thinking the same thing."

"Thanks for the information, Banks. Good work."

It appeared that Cassidy had even more reason than before to talk to the governor again.

There was no better time than now.

CASSIDY STOPPED by Governor Hollick's house, but he wasn't there. Neither was Peter.

Another guard had told her both men were on a fishing expedition.

Convenient.

Cassidy planned on tracking Hollick down the moment he got back, which would be later this evening. The guard had told her that much.

With that information tucked away for later, Cassidy went back to the office again.

Mac was waiting for her there. His eyes looked bright as if he had new information.

"I just got a call from someone who seems reputable," he announced.

Cassidy urged him to sit down in his normal spot across from her desk. "Who?"

"Her name is Venita Manchester. She's from the Charlotte area of North Carolina. She says that the girl you referred to as Janie is her great niece."

A lump formed in Cassidy's throat. "Tell me more."

"According to her, this girl—she said her name is Annabeth—"

"The same name that the couple who posed as her parents said it was."

"Exactly. She said that Annabeth and her family went on a ten-day vacation to the Bahamas four days ago. They wanted to go somewhere without any cell phones, where they couldn't be contacted."

Had that proved to be a fatal mistake?

Had something happened to the family on that trip?

Or had they not been telling the complete truth?

Cassidy licked her lips before asking, "What did she say about Annabeth?"

"Just that the girl is her great niece and that she wants to come pick her up."

Cassidy nodded. She'd figured that much. "I'm going to need to run her background information before I expose Janie—or Annabeth—to anyone, especially after the incident with the Shacklefords."

"That sounds reasonable."

Cassidy's mind continued to race. "When did Ms. Manchester say she was coming?"

"She said she'd drive over and that she'd leave right away. If she does that, I'm estimating she'll be here in six or seven hours."

"That gives me enough time to do a little research first." Cassidy wanted to be thorough here.

"That's what I thought. In the meantime, I'll keep taking these calls and see if anything else turns up." Mac rose and headed toward the door.

"One more thing," Cassidy said. "Did Ms. Manchester give you the names of Annabeth's parents?"

"Joe and Alexandria Manchester."

Cassidy jotted the names on a pad of paper on her desk. "They're based out of Charlotte also?"

"No, he's in Raleigh. He's a doctor there."

It looked like Cassidy knew exactly how she'd be spending the next couple of hours.

CHAPTER TWENTY-EIGHT

AFTER MAC LEFT, Cassidy began researching everything she could find about the Manchesters and Aunt Venita.

First, she found their pictures online.

Alexandria Manchester was a pretty brunette with a thin build and hair to her shoulders. Her husband also had dark hair and a trim build. The two of them looked truly happy together—all the way from their reserved smiles to their sparkling eyes.

She held her breath as she continued to scroll.

She wasn't sure what she was going to find.

She froze when she spotted a picture of the couple with a girl.

With Janie.

Or Annabeth.

In Cassidy's mind, the girl would forever be Janie now.

A frown tugged at her lips.

The family looked so happy in the photos. There were pictures of the three of them in a variety of places. In the tropics wearing bathing suits. In the mountains with ski gear on. In Paris with the Eiffel Tower behind them.

The family, by all appearances, had plenty of money.

Was that what this was about? Had someone snatched the child, hoping to blackmail the parents or request ransom? Had that happened while they were in the Bahamas?

Just what horrible event had happened to this family?

Out of curiosity, she looked into any other family members. It looked like Venita, who had never been married, had raised Joe after his parents abandoned him. Alexandria had come out of the foster care system.

Did they truly not have any other family but Venita? No one else had come forward yet.

Cassidy continued to scroll through everything she could find.

She wanted to know as much about the Manchesters as she could. Janie's life might depend on it.

In the middle of her research, her phone rang.

When she saw the number, her heart felt like it stopped for a moment.

It was her doctor up in Virginia.

He was most likely calling with the results of her tests.

She squeezed her eyes shut and prayed for good news.

AN HOUR LATER, Cassidy closed her computer and rubbed her eyes.

She wanted to forget about that phone call. She'd tried to work after speaking to the doctor.

But she couldn't.

The doctor's words played over and over again in her head until tears heated her eyes.

No, not here.

She'd have time to think about things later.

Right now, she had to concentrate on Janie. Concentrate on a child who needed her help.

Not on a child that had yet to be conceived.

Pulling in a deep breath, she reviewed her notes on the case.

From everything she could tell, this family, the Manchesters, appeared to be upstanding. She couldn't find a single bad thing about them online or through the background checks she did.

All the pictures made it seem that Janie truly was their daughter.

Cassidy had even seen a picture of somebody who'd been tagged as a Venita, the aunt who was headed this way.

But all that didn't give her any answers.

How had Annabeth ended up in the ocean with a life jacket with Cassidy's name on it? That made no sense.

And how did she and her family fit with the governor being in town?

That didn't make sense either.

Cassidy checked her watch and saw she still had four hours until Venita was to arrive in town.

The governor wasn't due back from his fishing expedition for another five hours.

That gave Cassidy entirely too much time on her hands.

There had to be something else she could do.

Her phone rang, and when she saw Ty's name on the screen, she quickly answered.

"What's going on?" she rushed.

"Cassidy, I just wanted to let you know that we saw a couple of people lingering near the Blackout headquarters."

Concern spread through her. "Did you catch them? Talk to them?"

"As soon as they realized we'd noticed them, they took off. They must have had a car close by because we couldn't catch them."

"Did you see the car?"

"I did," Ty said. "It was a black SUV."

"Noted." Cassidy frowned.

Just how many people were on this island who wanted to get to Janie?

She didn't know, but the very thought of it disturbed her.

CHAPTER TWENTY-NINE

CASSIDY WENT home to eat dinner and spend some time with Ty and Janie.

After they ate, Cassidy dreaded doing what she needed to do next.

But it couldn't be avoided.

With Janie situated on the couch with that teddy bear in her arms, Cassidy pulled up a picture on her phone—a picture of Venita Manchester.

She sat beside Janie on the couch and showed her the phone. "I know this might be hard, but do you recognize this woman?"

Cassidy braced herself, unsure if the girl would feel fear like she had after seeing the Shacklefords' picture or if she'd have a different reaction.

Janie's eyes widened, and she pointed at the photo.

Cassidy sucked in a breath.

The girl was responding.

This was a good step.

"Is this your great aunt? Venita?" Cassidy asked.

The girl looked at her, a new emotion in her eyes.

That was when Cassidy knew that this girl had recognized this woman. No fear presented itself in her gaze.

Once Venita arrived, if she checked out, then these two could be reunited.

Cassidy's heart sagged. She'd miss having Janie around. In the short time she'd been here, Cassidy had felt a bond with the girl.

Maybe Cassidy had understood the girl and her situation because of Cassidy's own subterfuge here on Lantern Beach.

Only two people on the island knew that her real name was Cady Matthews. Ty and Mac were the only ones who knew that a deadly gang had put a bounty on Cassidy's head after she'd accidentally killed their leader. She'd been a detective at the time.

Now, she could never return to her old life back in Seattle. Never.

Not that she ever wanted to. She was content here.

But things could turn around quickly.

Part of Cassidy wanted to keep this girl tucked away safe here at Blackout, just as Cassidy had kept herself safe by tucking away on Lantern Beach.

The world thought she was dead. Her murder and the media coverage of it had been staged. That fact had offered her some safety.

But sometimes she had to wonder just how long that would last.

She glanced at the time.

Venita was supposed to be here at any moment.

Cassidy needed to head back to the station to meet her.

But they would leave Janie here until they knew for sure that Venita was the one showing up. Cassidy couldn't take any chances—not when it came to Janie's safety.

BACK AT THE STATION, Cassidy glanced at her watch again.

Venita was an hour late.

Cassidy knew only one more ferry was coming

to the island tonight. If Venita didn't catch that one, then she wouldn't arrive until tomorrow morning.

Cassidy frowned at the thought.

Cassidy *could* send a boat over to pick the woman up from Ocracoke. But traversing these waters in the evening had its challenges. The ferry, with its channeled path, was the safest bet.

She needed to start thinking of a Plan B in case something went wrong here.

As she mulled things over, Mac leaned in her doorway. "Still nothing?"

Cassidy shook her head and took another sip of coffee. "I thought Venita Manchester would be here by now."

"I just tried to call her. She didn't answer."

Concern rose in Cassidy. That wasn't what she wanted to hear.

Why wouldn't the woman be answering her phone? Had this been another attempt to snatch Janie? What if Venita had never called—what if it had been another con-woman?

"Maybe she's out of range," Mac suggested.

"She could be." Service out here could be spotty at times. "Still, I don't like this."

Mac sat in the chair across from her. "I don't

either. But let's give her a little more time before we start digging into this more."

Unfortunately, Cassidy's patience was beginning to run thin.

She needed to focus her thoughts if she wanted to stay on top of things.

"Did you get any more interesting phone calls?" she asked Mac.

"We've had lots of phone calls. I've pretty much been busy all day. But very few of them offered any more information than what I told you. Other people have called and identified the girl as Annabeth Manchester, so I feel confident that's her name. They also corroborated the story Venita told us about the family going on a ten-day vacation to the Bahamas."

She tapped her pen against her desk. "Do you know if this was something they'd planned for a while?"

Mac's eyes glimmered. "Funny you ask. A few people made it sound like it was spontaneous."

"Were they a spontaneous type of family?"

"My impression? No. The doctor even had to cancel some of his appointments in order to make the trip happen."

The bad feeling continued to brew in Cassidy's

gut. "Something's wrong. I don't know what, but it's something."

"I agree. I don't like this."

Cassidy glanced at her watch again, her impatience—or was it a sense of urgency?—finally winning the battle. "I can't wait anymore. I'm going to follow up and see if Venita got on that last ferry. Then I'm going to call authorities in the Bahamas to see if they've seen the Manchesters. We have to figure out what's going on."

CHAPTER THIRTY

CASSIDY STOOD beside the superintendent of operations for the ferry from Ocracoke to Lantern Beach and reviewed the footage of all the cars being loaded onto the ferry.

But there was no record of Venita Manchester's car boarding that last one. Attendants wrote down every license plate on every trip.

Cassidy had looked through DMV records to find out what kind of car Venita drove. There *was* a possibility that she'd taken a different car—or maybe borrowed or rented one. But Cassidy figured that was the least likely scenario.

Besides, if Venita had caught this ferry—whatever car she was driving—where was she now? She hadn't come to the police station.

If Cassidy were in this woman's shoes, and Venita was worried about Annabeth as she claimed, it would seem she'd come right to the station to check on her niece.

Something was wrong.

Cassidy had already tried the woman's phone several times. There was no answer.

Whatever was going on, a part of Cassidy didn't want to know what.

Yet she had to know.

So much was on the line right now.

Too much.

She thanked the superintendent for his help before going to her car and heading to the station again.

Ty met her there.

He rose from his seat to meet her in her office. "What's the update?"

Cassidy shook her head in disbelief. They'd come so far . . . and now this. "It's like the woman has disappeared."

Ty's jaw tightened. "I don't like the way this is sounding."

"Neither do I. Either someone was trying to fool us again or something happened to her."

"Neither of which are good."

"No, they're not." Cassidy rolled her head over her shoulders, trying to work out the kinks there.

The stress of the situation was taking a toll on her body. Her head pounded, her eyelids were heavy, and other aches and pains had popped up.

Her doctor wouldn't approve.

Mac stepped into the room, a grim look on his face.

Cassidy braced herself for bad news.

"I put in a call with a few of my contacts with the North Carolina State Police," he started.

"And?" Cassidy held her breath.

"I discovered there's been a car accident. It looks like Venita was run off the road on the way here."

Cassidy's shoulders slumped, along with the rest of her muscles.

"And?" she asked.

Mac's frown deepened. "She's dead."

She sank deeper into her chair.

That hadn't been a coincidence.

Cassidy had no doubt in her mind about that.

Just why was someone so desperate to either cover up Janie's identity or to grab the girl for themselves? And how had they known Janie's aunt was on her way to Lantern Beach?

Had someone been keeping tabs on the aunt?

When she figured out those answers, everything else would fall into place.

But how many more people would die before that happened?

A FEW MINUTES LATER, Cassidy pulled her jacket back on.

That news had only made her determination grow.

"I'm going to go talk to the governor," Cassidy said. "Now. I can't wait any longer."

Ty followed behind her as she stepped toward the door. "I'm going with you."

Cassidy didn't argue. "I don't want to take any chances with this guy. Not until we know what he's up to."

She always felt better when she had Ty along. Just his presence alone was imposing. Sometimes, that really came in handy.

"Tread carefully," Mac called. "He could make your life miserable."

"His position doesn't intimidate me. Besides, I'm not going to back down to a bully."

"That's not what I want you to do. Not at all. I just

need you to remember that he has connections." Mac's words hung in the air.

Cassidy knew what he was getting at.

If the governor got nosy enough, he might discover who Cassidy really was. He could expose her.

But right now, Cassidy didn't even care. All that mattered was finding justice for this little girl and locating her parents.

If the governor had any information that would help this investigation, then he had an obligation to share it.

Cassidy and Ty climbed in her SUV and took off down the road again.

The governor should be back from his fishing expedition by now.

Irritation tightened her muscles at the thought of him enjoying himself out there while everything was going on.

Had he purposely left today, knowing he'd need an alibi? To try to take himself away from any potential questioning?

Because if that was the case, then he obviously didn't know Cassidy Chambers. She was going to do whatever it took to get to the bottom of this.

When she pulled up to the house where the

governor was staying, she saw two cars in the driveway.

Good. That should mean that he was here.

As she started toward the door, Ty grabbed her arm and tugged her back. "Don't make too many accusations unless you have evidence to back it up."

"But—"

"I know you feel strongly about this. And I don't blame you for that. But you don't want this guy to be your enemy. Mac is right."

Cassidy wanted to argue again, but she knew she shouldn't. Mac and Ty knew what they were talking about. Letting her emotions get the best of her right now would only lead to more frustration.

She drew in a deep breath, trying to calm her racing heart.

Then she looked back at the door and nodded. "I've got this. Let's see what Hollick has to say."

CHAPTER THIRTY-ONE

PETER'S NOSTRILS flared as he stared at Cassidy and Ty. "You're not welcome here without an appointment. I thought I'd made that clear."

"It's an urgent police matter. I need to speak to the governor." Cassidy felt Ty edging closer to her when he heard the man's oppressive tone.

"He's getting cleaned up from a fishing trip."

Cassidy crossed her arms. "Then I'll wait."

Finally, Peter opened the door wider and allowed them inside. "Wait here. Don't move. Don't touch anything or talk to anyone."

Cassidy was happy to have made it this far. She desperately needed to talk to Hollick, and she didn't like all the roadblocks that have been put in place—even if they were necessary.

As soon as Peter disappeared from sight, Cassidy leaned toward Ty and whispered, "He's a real peach, isn't he?"

"I've seen worse." Ty's gaze trailed after the man. "But as much as he's objecting, it's almost like he's covering up something."

"I agree."

Fifteen minutes later, the governor came downstairs. He wore black lounge pants and a long-sleeved T-shirt—far from his customary suit. His hair was wet as if he'd just gotten out of the shower.

But perhaps it was the scowl across his face that Cassidy noticed the most.

"I suppose I didn't make it clear when I said that this vacation was supposed to be about family time," he scolded as he approached.

"I understand, sir, and I do respect the boundaries that you put in place." Cassidy stood a little straighter. "But this is a police matter that can't wait."

He stopped in front of them, his beady gaze sliding from Cassidy to Ty and then back to Cassidy again. "You've got five minutes."

"That's all I'll need," Cassidy said. "When I talked to you before, I showed you the picture of that little girl."

A flash of irritation lit his gaze. "And I told you that I didn't recognize her."

"Yes, I know that." Cassidy remained unemotional as much as she could. "But some further evidence has come to light, and I really need to re-examine that issue."

He broke out of his stiff stance and shook his head. "Look, Chief, I'm really not sure what you think that has to do with me. I know a lot of strange things are going on here on the island. But I have nothing to do with them. The only people who know I'm here are the ones with me right now. So I don't really know what you're getting at."

She needed to defuse this situation before the governor totally shut her out. "That's what we are trying to figure out also. It seems like most of these crimes are somehow linked to your presence here on the island."

He scoffed. "Good luck trying to figure out what those links are. To me, it sounds like a coincidence."

He started to step away.

Cassidy couldn't lose him. Not now.

"Just one more question for you," Cassidy called. "Do the names Joe and Alexandria Manchester mean anything to you?"

As soon as she said the words, Hollick's face went pale. "Joe? I know Joe."

Cassidy's breath caught. "How do you know Joe?"

"He's my doctor."

"HAVE you ever had any trouble with him?" Cassidy continued.

In one way, the governor seemed to have relaxed more and, in another, he'd become more tense.

At least, now the man knew Cassidy wasn't totally off track. He also seemed to realize he could be in danger. That fact had finally sunk in. Maybe now she could get some answers from the guy.

The governor leaned back in a wingback chair. Peter stood in the background, listening to everything. Hollick had told him he could stay, though Cassidy wished the man would give them some breathing room. His main goal seemed to be to want to intimidate.

That wasn't going to work with either Cassidy or Ty.

"Joe is great," the governor started. "He's been my doctor since before I took office."

"And you didn't realize he had a daughter?" That didn't ring 100 percent true to Cassidy.

Hollick sighed, his expression showing a touch of regret. "I never really asked about his personal life. In general, it's better that I don't know. Besides, Joe seemed to like his privacy like I like my privacy. I could respect that."

She supposed that could be true. "When was the last time you saw Dr. Manchester?"

Hollick glanced at the window as if collecting his thoughts. "Probably about six months ago. That's about as often as I go to him. I'm trying to keep my cholesterol in check, which is why I see him that often. Plus, for my yearly checkups."

"Are you scheduled to see him anytime soon?" Ty asked.

"Next week. That's when I have my annual physical." Hollick froze and glanced at Cassidy, something close to fear on his features. "Do you think that has something to do with this?"

It was a possibility worth exploring.

"We're working hard to figure that out," Cassidy said, careful to remain vague until they had more details. "Since you said Dr. Manchester didn't talk very much about his private life, I don't suppose you know about any of his other family members?"

"Not really. Like I said, he was pretty quiet. He did mention that he liked to travel. He would get excited when he told me about trips he had coming up."

"I assume he had some type of background check in order to be your doctor because of your position," Cassidy continued.

"That's correct. But Joe passed with flying colors. There were no issues with him. Not at all." Hollick shrugged as if he were truly perplexed by the turn this case had taken.

"Thank you for your help." Cassidy stood and stepped toward the door, Ty following her lead.

"What does this mean?" Hollick rose, suddenly not as interested in making this conversation pass as quickly as possible.

"That's what we're trying to figure out," Cassidy said. "But in the meantime, I'd stay out of sight."

"We need to get him back to his home ASAP." Peter stepped forward, injecting his opinion as usual.

Cassidy turned to the governor as she answered. "I'm not sure that traveling is a good idea right now."

"Obviously, the safety here isn't up to par." Peter scowled. "I've been saying that the whole time."

Cassidy knew that he was trying to take another

dig at her. She ignored him, unwilling to give him that satisfaction.

"Until we have some more answers, I'd like to request that you stay close," she told the governor.

Hollick stared at her a moment, his gaze traversing side to side in thought. "I'll take that under consideration."

"But his safety is our first priority." Peter stepped closer. "It doesn't matter what you say. Nothing will change my mind on that."

Cassidy felt Ty bristle beside her.

She pushed a hand back, letting him know she could handle this.

Then she leveled her gaze with Peter.

"Understood. But you also need to understand that nobody is above the law here." She narrowed her eyes so she could drive home her point. "Nobody."

CHAPTER THIRTY-TWO

"THAT WAS AN INTERESTING CONVERSATION," Ty said as they headed away from the governor's house.

"Wasn't it, though?"

Cassidy had handed him the keys to her SUV as soon as they'd stepped outside. Ty knew she was too upset to drive—if she had a choice in the matter.

He could see that the stress of this case was beginning to get to her—and that worried him.

At least she had let him come along. But now his mind raced through what they'd just learned.

"So what are we missing here?" Cassidy leaned back in the seat and closed her eyes. "We have a missing doctor and his wife. That doctor treats the governor. The people who were staying in the house beside the governor were found dead. The doctor's daughter came ashore in a life jacket with my name on it."

"Don't forget about the bag full of alcohol swabs from the pharmaceutical company."

"There's that also. Finding that bag *could* be a coincidence, just like the company head said."

Yes, it could be.

But Ty was trained in tactical warfare. This battle they were fighting right now might not be on enemy territory, but there had definitely been some figurative bombs hidden.

He just had to figure out which areas were dangerous and which were safe.

Right now, everything seemed like a potential explosion.

"Something bad is going on here, Cassidy," Ty finally said. "Maybe someone wants so badly to get their hands on Janie simply because they want to get to her dad."

"What would they want Joe Manchester to do?"

"He has direct access to the governor . . ." As the words hung in the air, Ty felt his gut clench. A lot of bad scenarios could happen in a situation like this. That was certain.

As he glanced in his rearview mirror, his shoulders tightened.

Cassidy turned her neck and followed his gaze. "What's going on?"

"A black car is behind us. They're driving close."

Just as he said the words, a bullet flew through the air and shattered the back window.

"Get down!" Ty yelled.

He tightened his grip on the steering wheel and hit the accelerator.

He couldn't believe somebody was shooting at them, especially in public.

If they weren't careful, there could be an innocent casualty.

Ty couldn't let that happen.

But he couldn't let his wife get hurt either.

As another bullet pierced the air, Ty pressed the accelerator harder. He had to lead this guy away from any civilians.

Then he needed to figure out who was driving that car.

CASSIDY GRIPPED the armrest beside her as Ty charged down the road.

These people were getting brazen.

It was the first time they'd done something so blatantly obvious.

That must mean that she was getting closer to the truth.

But Cassidy would have to think through those details later. Right now, she and Ty had to concentrate on surviving.

Another bullet flew through the air, this one hitting the front windshield.

As it shattered, shards of glass rained down on them.

Ty started to swerve but quickly righted the vehicle.

Cassidy was thankful he was driving. He was better in these situations than she was. Waging war in the Middle East did that to a person, she supposed.

"Ty, where are you going?" She gripped the armrest more tightly as wind flooded into the vehicle, sending a frigid message.

"To the lighthouse," he said. "There shouldn't be anybody out there."

He was probably right, but . . . what would they do when they got there? Would these guys continue to hunt them down?

Cassidy had a gun on her. She had no doubt that Ty also had his.

But she had no idea who—or what—they were up against.

As the houses faded around them and the area became more wooded, Cassidy grabbed her phone. She called in backup. Bradshaw and Banks promised they were on their way.

Not much longer, and they'd be at the lighthouse.

Cassidy remained low, watching for any incoming bullets. But it was Ty she was worried about. He couldn't crouch but so low and still drive.

Dear Lord . . . help us now!

All she could do was mutter the prayer over and over again.

Another bullet whizzed past them.

These guys weren't giving up.

Thinking about something happening to Ty made Cassidy's heart twist into knots. Despite the challenges they faced now, they still had so much life left to do together. Things couldn't end this way.

Finally, they reached the end of the road.

Ty hit the brakes, and the SUV swerved around in a half circle, screeching to a stop in front of their attackers.

Cassidy held her breath as she waited to see how things would play out.

They were at a face-off.

And their next moves could mean life or death.

CHAPTER THIRTY-THREE

CASSIDY STARTED to climb from the SUV with her gun drawn. Ty placed a hand on her arm to stop her.

"Just wait," he murmured.

He must sense something that she didn't.

She stared at the black SUV, the same one that had been spotted earlier on the island near the Blackout complex.

It was dark outside, and the windows were tinted. Cassidy couldn't see who was inside.

She only knew that whoever was driving the car was dangerous.

The wind swept around them, coming through the broken windshield again.

Cassidy repressed a shudder.

She could hardly breathe as she waited. As she anticipated how she should react.

Her hand remained on her gun. She'd pull the trigger if she had to.

But she hoped it didn't come to that.

The other car roared to life.

It swerved around them before rushing away.

"We've got to go after them!" Cassidy said.

Ty threw the SUV into Drive, and they charged after the vehicle.

They couldn't let them get away.

But the next instant, something flew from the car's window.

Before Ty could stop, they hit the object.

Pop! Pop! Pop!

Their SUV lurched and groaned before sputtering to a stop.

Cassidy's heart pounded out of control.

She glanced at Ty.

He was okay.

"What happened?" Cassidy rushed.

Ty's gaze darkened and his jaw clenched as he threw the SUV into Park. "They must have thrown out a tack strip. They were waiting for us and ready for whatever would happen."

Cassidy felt tension seize her body.

She couldn't let them get away.

But it looked like that was exactly what was going to happen.

CASSIDY AND TY went back to the station long enough to update everybody on what was going on. Her officers had found the SUV abandoned in the woods.

They would run its plates, but Cassidy knew that whoever was behind this was too smart to let them chase them this way. No doubt this vehicle had been stolen and wouldn't lead them to the people behind this.

Finally, Ty and Cassidy headed back to the Blackout complex to spend time with Janie.

But when they got there, the girl was already sleeping in her bed, totally unaware of today's events.

CJ, another of Blackout's recruits, sat cross-legged in the living room, looking at a magazine. She rose when Ty and Cassidy came in.

"She's been great," CJ said. "No problems."

"Good to know," Cassidy said. "Thank you so much for your help."

"It was almost as much fun as giving Benjamin a hard time." She winked. "Let me know if you need more help."

As CJ left, Cassidy studied Janie's peaceful figure.

Her heart warmed at the sight of her. The girl had no idea what had transpired today. Janie had thought that a relative was coming to pick her up.

Would she be disappointed in the morning when she found out her aunt hadn't come?

Cassidy's heart lurched at the thought of it.

The poor girl. She was entirely too young to have to go through all this.

Ty wrapped his arms around Cassidy's waist as they stared at Janie together.

"She looks so serene, doesn't she?" he whispered.

"She does. I'm glad. It's going to be a tough road for her, no matter what happens in the future."

"It will. But humans are more resilient than we give ourselves credit for. She'll bounce back."

"I just hope she gets a happy ending."

Ty nuzzled the side of her neck. "I hope you get your happy ending too, Cassidy."

She turned in his arms to face him. "You're my happy ending."

Ty grinned softly, almost sadly. Emotions swirled

in his eyes, his compassion running much deeper than most people would ever assume.

"I appreciate that. But I know there's more you want also."

Cassidy stepped back. She hadn't told him about the doctor's phone call yet. She didn't want to do it now. Didn't want to break this moment.

But there would never be a good time to share the news.

"Dr. Kincaid called," she started.

Ty went still. "And?"

"He said . . ." She drew in a deep breath, trying to remain strong. "He said that I have what's called a diminished ovarian reserve."

"What's that mean?"

"That my body doesn't produce enough eggs for me to get pregnant the old-fashioned way."

Disappointment filled his gaze. "Oh, Cassidy . . . I'm sorry. Did he say anything else? Is there anything we can try?"

She shrugged, still feeling on the verge of losing it. She didn't want Ty to know how much this had broken her. If she let herself feel everything now, she might not be able to pull herself together enough to concentrate on this case.

"He said we could always do an IUI followed by a few rounds of IVF."

"I have to admit, I don't know much about either of those things."

"IVF would require hormonal shots and embryo transfers and . . . aside from all that, it's costly. Very costly." Ty's position with Hope House was mostly a labor of love. They'd never had to worry about money in the past. But they'd never faced a big expense like this either.

"Doing that would require more trips up to Virginia." Worry pooled in his eyes. "That's more risk of exposure for you. Every time you leave this island—"

"I put myself in danger of having the wrong person recognize me." She nodded. She'd already thought of that. "I know."

Ty didn't say anything for a minute. "What do you want to do?"

"I'm not sure yet."

"Then let's pray about it." Ty reached for Cassidy's face and ran his thumb down her cheek. "We need to keep believing that God's plan for our future is the right plan."

"I know." Her voice cracked. "But sometimes the waiting is so hard."

"But waiting is worth it. God's proved that time and time again."

Cassidy nodded, his words a gentle reminder to her.

He was right.

The two of them were going to get through this.

And, in the end, they'd only be stronger—whether their arms were empty or full.

Despite the reassurance, the wisdom . . . a sob escaped Cassidy at the thought.

CHAPTER THIRTY-FOUR

CASSIDY SPENT the next morning at the station, reviewing information and seeing if she could find out any updates.

She'd stationed Officer Banks outside the governor's house last night. When she'd checked with him, he'd told her he hadn't seen anything out of sorts. Everyone had stayed put, and no suspicious cars had come past.

The SUV they'd found—the one used to chase her and Ty—had been stolen from a dealership in Virginia. Cassidy had obtained footage of the vehicle pulling onto the ferry. But the driver had never put his window down or stepped out, so she had no idea what the person inside looked like.

Venita Manchester had passed away from

injuries sustained in the car accident. It appeared she'd been intentionally run off the road, but the police had no suspects yet.

All the pieces of the puzzle were in front of her.

Now Cassidy needed to figure out exactly how to put them together.

Near lunchtime, she grabbed her laptop and headed to The Crazy Chefette. She needed something to eat. She also liked to keep a pulse on the people here in town. Sometimes going to local eating establishments was the best way to study the people coming and going from the island.

She set up a little makeshift office in a corner booth before ordering a grilled cheese and peach sandwich, her favorite.

As she nibbled on it, she began to research Buxton Pharmaceuticals.

She knew the company probably had nothing to do with this situation, but she needed to explore every possibility right now. This was no time to slack off or make assumptions.

"How's everything going?" Lisa asked as she strode up to her table.

Cassidy leaned back and let out a breath. "They've been better, to be honest. But we're going to figure out everything that's been happening here."

Lisa glanced at Cassidy's computer, and her eyes widened with recognition. "I've seen that man before."

Cassidy glanced at the screen. "That's Richard Robertson, the CEO of the pharmaceutical company."

Lisa tapped on her lips with her finger as she thought. "Where I have seen him?"

Cassidy didn't say anything. Instead, she waited to hear what her friend came up with.

Suddenly, Lisa's eyes lit. "I know! He was in here about two months ago."

"This guy was? Richard Robertson?"

"That's right. How could I forget? He was very difficult and kept sending all the food back. The hamburger was too overcooked. The sauce was too spicy. He liked his bread to be toasted." She rolled her eyes. "That's probably the only reason that I remember him. Plus, he didn't exactly look like a fisherman or the usual tourist we get in here this time of the year."

"You're absolutely sure?" Cassidy clarified.

"I'm positive. I'd remember that angular face anywhere."

Cassidy bit down.

It looked like another lead had risen to the

surface.

She needed to get busy because time was running out.

CASSIDY RESEARCHED everything she could about Richard Robertson.

On the surface, he looked like an upstanding guy. The CEO of a successful pharmaceutical company. Widowed. No children. Active in the nonprofit community.

Cassidy knew from their earlier conversation that some of the funding he'd had for a project had been pulled by the government.

Was that enough to make this man target the governor, who'd once served at the NIH?

And what did this have to do with the governor's doctor and that same doctor's daughter?

The thoughts continued to churn inside Cassidy's head.

As she scrolled through Richard's social media posts, she paused at an obituary.

Her pulse quickened.

Richard's wife had died six months ago.

Cassidy clicked on the link and continued looking until she found more information.

The man's wife had died from ALS.

She paused and let that sink in.

The funding that had been pulled from the pharmaceutical company was for a new drug they thought could cure that disease.

When the government had pulled support, had that solidified this woman's death sentence?

Cassidy's heart pounded in her ears as she leaned back in her chair, letting that sink in.

Could she really be onto something?

Her gut told her yes.

But now she needed to prove it.

She called Dillinger and asked him to pinpoint Robertson's last known location, based on cell phone records and credit card usage. She knew it would take him at least an hour to get anything back, if not longer.

In the meantime, she continued scrolling through the pictures.

This Robertson guy would have to be really desperate to go through all this trouble. And Cassidy still wasn't sure exactly why the girl had been found on the beach wearing the life jacket with Cassidy's name on it.

But a clearer picture came together in her mind—clearer but even more disturbing.

Cassidy called Mac and Ty to give them the updates on the situation.

Just as she reached the end of those calls, her phone rang.

Dillinger.

"Chief, you'll never believe this." Excitement rose in his voice. "This Richard Robertson guy . . . his cell phone hasn't pinged in two weeks. But the last time it did . . . he was on Lantern Beach."

CHAPTER THIRTY-FIVE

AS DILLINGER and Bradshaw tried to locate Robertson on the island, Cassidy went to talk to the governor.

It was clear he was no longer safe here on the island.

And she would talk to the governor with or without Peter's permission.

Several minutes later, she pounded at Hollick's door, and his head of security answered, greeting her with a scowl.

"What are you doing here again?" His voice held an edge of arrogance.

Cassidy raised her chin, refusing to break her gaze or back down to this man. "I need to speak to the governor."

"About what?"

"I'm afraid that's private."

The man's scowl deepened, and he started to close the door. "Then I can't help you."

She raised her hand and stopped the door.

"What do you think you're doing?" he growled.

Cassidy was beginning to wonder if this guy might have something to do with all these incidents. He was certainly controlling. Good guy or bad guy, this guy was letting his pride get in the way of his duty.

"Sir, I'm not going to ask you again." Cassidy hardened her voice. "I need to speak to the governor about an urgent matter."

He stared at her again, his chest puffing with anger.

But before he could argue with her more, a figure appeared in the background.

Governor Hollick.

"Chief." He started toward her, wrinkles forming at the corners of his eyes. "What brings you by again?"

Cassidy stepped around Peter. As she did, she felt the tension coming off him in waves.

"Governor, something urgent has come to my attention," Cassidy started. "We need to talk."

"Very well." He nodded to Peter. "I'd like some privacy."

"But that's—"

"No arguments." Hollick pressed his lips together, decision made.

After a moment of hesitation, Peter cast another dirty look at Cassidy before walking away, leaving a cool breeze in his wake.

The governor motioned for Cassidy to take a seat beside him in the sitting area near the door. She lowered herself onto the couch, careful to stay close so they could speak without being overheard.

The governor had an inclination about why she was here, didn't he?

This whole conversation was going to be interesting.

And it would most likely hold a lot of answers she needed.

Cassidy closed her eyes for just a moment before she started.

Lord, give me the right words. Please.

A little girl's life might depend on it.

CASSIDY CLEARED her throat before starting. "Governor, because of the new information that I've discovered, I'm not sure if Lantern Beach is the safest place for you to be."

His gaze darkened. "What new information?"

"We've been looking into your ties with Buxton Pharmaceuticals."

His eyes narrowed just slightly—enough to indicate that she'd hit on something.

"Have you?" he asked.

"We discovered that the man who filed the lawsuit against you has been spotted here on Lantern Beach within the past couple of weeks."

The governor's face dropped two shades of white. "Richard Robertson?"

At least Hollick hadn't denied it. "He's the one. It seems the man has quite the beef with you."

Hollick rolled one of his shoulders back before his gaze met Cassidy's. "Do you think Robertson has something to do with what's been happening here?"

"That's what we're trying to figure out. Can you tell me, in your own words, about that whole situation?"

Hollick drew in a deep breath and stared out the window a moment. "There's not much to tell. Robertson was trying to develop a drug for ALs, and another company came along with more effective research and testing. The other company ended up with the funding."

"You made that decision?"

"It was based off my recommendation. The government's money isn't just a free-for-all. When I worked in my role with the National Institutes of Health, we had to be very particular how we handed out our funding. Despite contrary belief, we didn't have a never-ending supply."

Cassidy soaked in every detail the governor shared, not wanting to miss a thing. "And what was wrong with the medication that Buxton Pharmaceuticals was developing?"

Hollick let out a long breath, as if the topic almost burdened him. "They weren't able to prove their results through any type of testing. Robertson really believed they were going to find a miracle cure for ALS. But based on all the research I read, they were nowhere close. They were throwing whatever they could at the wall and hoping something would stick, so to speak."

Cassidy paused before asking her next question. "You realize that Robertson's wife had ALS, which could have been part of the reason he was pushing so hard to find a cure?"

The governor nodded, the wrinkles on his face seeming to grow deeper. "I did realize that. I also felt that was part of the reason Robertson was blinded by those very results. He was so desperate to help her that he believed his team was on the right track. But they weren't."

Cassidy squared her shoulders before launching into her next question, knowing it may not be received well. But she'd come this far. She couldn't stop now.

"So when you pulled their funding, it had nothing to do with the fact that your brother's pharmaceutical company ended up getting that research grant?" Her question hung in the air.

Hollick's eyes narrowed even more, and Cassidy knew he didn't appreciate the insinuation. She'd had no choice but to ask.

"That had nothing to do with it," Hollick said. "And, yes, my brother is on the board of directors for that pharmaceutical company. But that doesn't mean he got any type of financial benefit from me giving them that grant. *That* would be a conflict of interest, something I'm morally opposed to."

"Nobody had a problem with the decision then?"

Hollick tugged his collar. "No, no one even noticed—because I didn't do anything wrong."

Tugging his collar? That was a sign that he very well *could* have done something wrong. It was his "tell," so to speak.

"After that happened, Richard Robertson filed a civil lawsuit against you," Cassidy continued. "That couldn't have made you happy."

The governor straightened, his tone suddenly brisk and his actions guarded. His gaze pierced into her, challenge rising up from the depths of his eyes. "Are you interrogating me, Chief?"

Back down, Cassidy. Don't push too hard.

The governor wasn't above the law, but he *did* need to be handled with a special kind of care and respect.

Cassidy held her ground. "No, sir. I'm just trying to find answers and keep a little girl safe. A little girl who is the daughter of your personal doctor. Don't you see that you're the connection here?"

He slumped before running a hand over his face. "That's what I've been afraid of. What can I do?"

CHAPTER THIRTY-SIX

CASSIDY MADE plans to evacuate the governor from the island. But it wasn't going to be easy on such short notice. The good news was that he'd already sent his wife and son back that morning. They'd had an event for his son's school that they didn't want to miss.

Meanwhile, Cassidy was coordinating with Blackout to help with Hollick's departure.

It was clear Hollick would be safer somewhere else right now—most likely in his own home with his state-of-the-art security system.

The governor had agreed with her assessment and asked her to lead the charge to get him off the island.

Cassidy remained at Hollick's as she coordinated

efforts, setting up a work area at his dining room table while Peter scowled at her at every chance he got.

She ignored him.

Meanwhile, the governor's staff was already packing up in anticipation of leaving.

Peter's negative energy seemed to crawl across the room and pinch each of Cassidy's nerves.

Finally, he said, "I should have been consulted."

His voice was full of accusation.

He knew he'd failed the governor, and he wasn't handling it well.

"Whatever you're talking about, that's a matter between you and the governor." Cassidy stared at the island map again, trying to ignore him. "I don't have time for these turf wars."

"I'm sure you don't." Tension stretched through his voice.

Enough!

Cassidy turned to Peter, unable to hold back the anger flashing in her eyes. "Look, I don't know why you have a problem with me. We both have the same goal—to keep the governor safe. I'd think you would welcome my help, but instead you're so busy trying to make sure you stay in control that you're focusing on the wrong things at the wrong time."

Peter's eyes mollified—but only for a moment. "I want to do a good job. I want the governor to know that when he took a chance on hiring me that it was a good choice."

There it was . . . insecurity that had been disguised as arrogance.

Cassidy kept her voice firm. "Then do a good job. Help me, instead of standing in my way."

His shoulders softened like a soldier who'd just been told, "At ease." "What do you need?"

Cassidy pointed to the map. "I think the helicopter coming to escort the governor back home should land at the Blackout complex. The location is more secure."

He raised his nose before agreeing. "It sounds like a good idea."

"But I want to make sure that Governor Hollick has an entourage to escort him to the location. These guys shot at us. Threw down a tack strip to stop our car. They possibly kidnapped a little girl and killed innocent civilians. We can't take any chances."

Cassidy halfway expected the man to argue.

Instead, Peter nodded. "I'll talk to the rest of my team. Then we'll coordinate with you on our next steps."

Relief flooded through her. At least she had his cooperation now. "Sounds good."

As they wrapped up the conversation, Cassidy glanced out the window. She saw a man and woman walking their greyhound down the street.

This was the second time that she'd seen the trio near the governor's place. They'd been outside last time she was here also, but nothing about them had raised any red flags.

Cassidy turned to Peter. "I'll be right back."

She wanted to talk to them.

But she had to hurry if she was going to catch them.

"EXCUSE ME!" Cassidy ran after the couple, her shoes hitting the gravel road and the rocks crunching beneath her.

The man and woman stopped and turned to her. As they did, their dog pulled at the leash and tried to jump on Cassidy.

"Down, Lightning." The man tugged at the leash, pulling his canine back. "Don't worry. He'll knock you over but only because he wants to lick your face. He's harmless."

Cassidy let Lightning sniff her hand. Once the dog gave his approval, she patted his head and turned back to the couple. She quickly introduced herself.

Bob and Lynn—probably in their early sixties—were lean and tall, much like their dog. Cassidy didn't recognize them, so she assumed they were vacationers. She knew most of the locals by now.

"I'm investigating a crime that took place here on the island," Cassidy started. "I noticed you two walking past here yesterday also. Is this a daily thing?"

"Every day." A touch of pride rang in the man's voice. "My wife and I like to walk at nine in the morning and six at night. It's good for the body to get some exercise, especially as you get older."

"If you don't mind me asking, when did you get into town?"

"Five days ago," Lynn said, her honey-blonde ponytail blowing in the breeze. "Why?"

"I'm wondering if, as you were walking, you saw anything out of the ordinary at either of these two houses." Cassidy nodded toward the governor's rental and then at the house where the Taylors had been killed.

"Anything out of the ordinary?" Bob let out a

little murmur to indicate he was thinking. "I'm not sure what really qualifies as out of the ordinary."

"Have you seen anything? Any movement at all?" Cassidy clarified.

His gaze met hers. "I've seen you over there a couple of times. But not much else, I don't guess."

"What about the other house?" Cassidy nodded at the Taylor's place.

"It's been pretty quiet this week, other than when the police were there a few days ago." Bob leaned down and rubbed his dog's head.

The man was obviously observant. Cassidy hoped that worked in her favor.

"What about before that?" Cassidy continued. "Did you see anything then?"

They were quiet a moment until Lynn snapped her fingers. "We *did* see a man and a woman pull in and begin to unload their things. Remember, honey? They were laughing and seemed so happy."

Cassidy's breath caught. "Can you tell me about that? Did you talk to them?"

Lynn shrugged. "They seemed friendly enough. Even waved hello to us. Told us they like birdwatching. I should have guessed—they had binoculars around their necks."

"Is that right?" Cassidy stored that information away. She hadn't heard that yet.

"As we were walking that evening, we saw some people crouching in the dunes near their house," Bob said. "Actually, Lightning saw them and started barking."

"We figured the couple had made friends already," Lynn said. "These other people had binoculars too."

Cassidy's pulse continued to quicken. Maybe she was finally onto something. "Can you describe the people you saw near the house?"

"It was a man and a woman—husband and wife, I assumed." Lynn shrugged. "They were dressed casually, like vacationers. Honestly, there wasn't anything remarkable about them."

A man *and* a woman?

The Shacklefords maybe?

Her breath caught. "And that's all?"

Cassidy hoped these people might have more to say. But she was thankful for all they'd already shared.

Bob shrugged. "That was it. The next morning the police were all over there. It's a crying shame that something like that would happen here on this island. It's definitely made us want to lock our doors at night."

Cassidy thanked them, then got their names and numbers. She gave them her card in case they thought of anything else also.

But it looked like the man and woman who'd been visiting the Taylors could very well be the killers.

Were those people the Shacklefords?

It was Cassidy's best guess.

CHAPTER THIRTY-SEVEN

"SO THE TAYLORS WERE BIRDWATCHERS." Cassidy had pulled Banks outside to give him the update.

She didn't want the governor to know too much—not until she'd had a chance to fact-check Bob and Lynn's statements. Throwing out theories could hurt her credibility.

Banks glanced at the large rental where the governor was staying. "Or were they spying on Hollick?"

Cassidy raised a shoulder in a half shrug. "I don't think they were. But we'd be wise to keep our mind open to possibilities."

"Let's say these people were innocent, and they did just come to Lantern Beach to look for piping plovers." Banks squinted as if confused by the very thought of it. "If that's the case, I can't see the connection between them, the governor, and a motive for killing them."

He raised a good point. "This other couple—Bob and Lynn—said they saw the Taylors with binoculars. We didn't find any of those at the crime scene, did we?"

"I can double-check, but I'm nearly certain that we didn't."

Cassidy shook her head and lifted her face to the breeze, thankful for the temperate day. "I don't think so either. I think the Taylors were looking for birds on the shore when they saw something they shouldn't have."

Banks's eyes widened before he nodded. "And you think they were killed for it?"

"I do. I don't know what they saw or any of the details, but that's my working theory."

"You think it had something to do with the governor?"

Cassidy looked back at Hollick's house. "It's the only thing that makes sense."

"What could they have seen? Someone bugging the house before the governor came?"

That was a good question. "We examined the

interior before the governor arrived and didn't find any bugs or anything else that caused alarm."

"So what else could someone be doing over at the governor's place—what else worth killing over?" Banks asked.

Cassidy mulled that question over. "Maybe they were just scoping it out, trying to get a feel for the layout of the place. Maybe they were planning to break in."

Banks shrugged, not bothering to hide his uncertainty. "Maybe. But that almost seems too simple."

Cassidy knew she had to wrap this conversation up soon and get back inside to talk to the rest of the team—including the governor's security detail. "Do you have another theory?"

"I wish I did." Banks glanced at his watch. "When does the governor plan on leaving?"

"His helicopter is going to be here in two hours. We don't want to get him to the site too early."

Banks glanced at her again. "You really think somebody's watching right now, just waiting to bombard him when he leaves?"

"At this point, I wouldn't put anything past these guys." She truly wouldn't.

And that's what scared her.

"And by 'these guys,' you mean the CEO of a pharmaceutical company?" Banks clarified.

"He's the one. I'm nearly certain he could have afforded to hire the Shacklefords to do his dirty work. He sent them to get Janie. There are still a lot of details to figure out. But we will. Right now, we need to concentrate on making sure that the governor is safe."

"Will do. I'm going to stand guard here and not let anyone come or go until you tell me it's okay."

"That sounds great." She tapped Banks's arm before pulling her cell phone out. "Keep up the good work."

As she took a step away, she put her phone to her ear. She needed to call Ty and check on Janie.

RELIEF WASHED through Ty when he heard Cassidy's voice on the phone.

He'd been managing the governor's evacuation from this side—talking to Colton and the gang about how they could help.

But he'd also been with Janie, trying to keep any of those conversations quiet so they wouldn't frighten the girl.

"It's been crazy," Cassidy said. "How's Janie?"

Ty glanced at Janie as she sat beside him at the kitchen table. She munched on some carrots in between coloring a picture.

Things felt surprisingly normal—even when it wasn't.

"She's doing fine," Ty said. "She's been playing with Ada some."

"I'm glad." Cassidy's voice caught. "Hopefully, this will all be over soon."

Ty hoped that as well. He wasn't sure if Cassidy could handle the stress of this situation for much longer.

On second thought, she *could* handle it. But what kind of toll would it take on her?

"Do you think all this will end once the governor is off the island?" Ty asked.

"I feel like he's been the target here this whole time, so let's hope."

Ty lowered his voice. "If that's true, then why was someone trying to grab Janie?"

Ty's question hung in the air.

Cassidy didn't say anything for a moment. "That's what we're trying to figure out. It must have something to do with her father, Dr. Manchester. But maybe once the governor is gone these people will leave Janie alone."

He glanced at Janie again—at her innocent face.

He only wished she'd speak. Then she could tell them what was going through her mind. If only he knew how to get her to talk.

"Stay safe, Cassidy. I don't like the sound of this." Concern threaded through Ty's voice.

"I'll see you later."

They ended the call.

As Ty watched Janie color a picture, he couldn't stop thinking about what Cassidy had told him last night.

About the fact that they may not be able to have a child without medical intervention.

He wasn't opposed to getting help if they needed it. But there were so many other factors involved. Money. Travel. Risk of exposure.

And then there was also the fact that it might not work.

Ty had known plenty of couples who'd gone through the process only to have spent thousands of dollars and still be childless.

He and Cassidy could just focus on adoption. He wasn't opposed to that either.

Mostly, what he wanted was to see the light

return to Cassidy's gaze. He could tell she was trying to be strong. But her chin had quivered as she'd spoken last night.

And then that sob had escaped.

Beneath her tough exterior, she was hurting inside.

That thought broke his heart.

All he'd known to do was hold her. He'd tried to find the right words of comfort, but there were none.

He turned his attention back to the present. Janie worked adamantly to color the petals of a pink daisy on her page. For a six-year-old, she was detailed with her work, careful to stay within the lines.

"You're doing a great job," he murmured. "I love the colors you picked out."

The girl looked up at him, and something close to a smile tugged at her lips.

Ty didn't know what the future held for this girl, but he prayed for only good things. The girl was obviously bright. But she had gone through something horrific, something that he couldn't even imagine.

He knew how events like that could affect people. He'd worked with people who'd experienced PTSD plenty of times. He'd been through war zones himself.

A six-year-old shouldn't have to experience any of those things. Yet, in many ways, the situations were the same. The *effects* were the same.

He hoped Cassidy was right and that once the governor was off the island that some of the trouble that had been haunting them lately would disappear.

But there were no guarantees.

Ty glanced at Janie again as she colored her picture. She'd moved to the edge of the paper and started to scribble something freehand in the corner.

"You decided to go rogue, huh? Do your own thing? I can respect that." Ty leaned closer to get a better look, assuming she was probably drawing a flower to fit with the forest scene.

What he saw caused him to flinch.

It was the same picture of the man and the woman Janie had drawn in an earlier picture.

Only this time, she'd clearly drawn tears coming from both of their eyes.

CHAPTER THIRTY-EIGHT

AN HOUR LATER, the security team was ready to go.

Four members would ride with Hollick—the men he'd brought with them. Two vehicles from Blackout had also joined them, one leading the procession and one bringing up the rear. Cassidy and Dillinger would follow in the vehicle directly behind the governor.

By the time everyone made it to the Blackout complex, they should have thirty minutes until the helicopter arrived to take the governor back to Raleigh.

Cassidy felt confident that all the elements were in place for a safe transport, but that didn't stop the nerves from rumbling inside her.

So much could still go wrong. Even though her team had covered every detail more than once, a lot of unknowns still existed.

She stared out the window as Dillinger drove down the road. As they traveled, she surveyed the area around them, looking for any signs of trouble.

So far, there was nothing.

But it would take at least ten minutes to get to the Blackout complex.

Those ten minutes were going to feel like ten hours.

"Do you think these guys are waiting to ambush us?" Dillinger stared at the road ahead, his posture more upright than usual.

Cassidy frowned. "I wouldn't put anything past them at this point."

"What do you think their end game is? Do you think they want to hurt the governor?"

"I'm not sure if these people want to hurt him, teach him a lesson, or convince him to see things their way. And when I say *their* I really mean *his*. I'm convinced all this goes back to Richard Robertson."

"What about the Shacklefords?" Dillinger asked.

"This guy has the means to hire people to do some of his dirty work."

Dillinger frowned again. "We checked all over the island. Nobody has seen them."

She'd figured that would be the case—unfortunately. "What about whoever was driving the SUV, the ones who fired at Ty and me yesterday? Were there any signs of them?"

"Nothing." Dillinger's jaw tensed as he shook his head. "And that's the thing. This island is only so big. We should have found them."

He was absolutely correct. "You and I both know that criminals can be creative. There's no telling what these people have done. As much as we've searched every inch of this island, we both know it's impossible to disappear like that."

Dillinger frowned. "If something happens to the governor . . ."

"Then this place is going to be all over the news." As Cassidy said the words, a sick feeling formed in her stomach.

There would be no way she could avoid the media scrutiny if that happened.

That meant that there was more on the line here than just the governor. Her future was at stake here too.

She and Ty had a lot that they needed to figure out. They'd never been promised tomorrow. But

Cassidy still had hopes and dreams that she didn't want to give up. The truth was, she wanted to grow old with Ty. Wanted to have a family. Wanted to create the life she'd never had growing up.

Finally, Cassidy and Dillinger pulled into the Blackout complex.

Cassidy released her breath as soon as they were inside the gate.

Maybe she'd been worked up about nothing. Maybe these guys really were somehow gone from the island.

The caravan stopped at an empty field where a helicopter would land in thirty minutes.

Cassidy climbed from the SUV and glanced around, surveying the area for any signs of trouble. The main building stood in the distance, a good half a mile away. The water stretched beyond that. Woods surrounded the fringe of the property.

She should feel at peace.

The quiet should soothe her.

But instead she still felt unnerved.

Was trouble lurking just out of sight?

RIGHT ON TIME, the governor's helicopter landed.

Cassidy released her breath. Maybe all this worry had been for nothing.

But she couldn't let her guard down yet. Too much was at stake.

She waited for the blades to stop spinning before approaching the aircraft. When it was clear, she and Peter nodded to each other before escorting the governor toward the copter.

Cassidy kept one hand near her gun just in case.

She hoped it didn't come to that.

The guys from Blackout remained on the lookout, even monitoring the woods surrounding the property. There weren't that many places to hide here—which made it an ideal location.

No surprises.

In theory, at least.

As soon as the governor was in the copter, he should be good to go. Another team would meet him in Raleigh and take over his detail from there.

As they reached the copter, the door opened and the pilot stepped out.

Cassidy's eyes widened when she saw the man.

The pilot was . . .

She blinked.

Richard Robertson?

She sucked in a breath.

Robertson wasn't alone. He pulled someone out behind him, clutching the man's arm. His other hand gripped a . . . gun.

He had taken someone hostage.

Cassidy drew her weapon just as members of the security team scrambled into action.

As Cassidy stared at the man Richard had brought with him, she let out a gasp.

She'd seen this man before.

In a photo.

It was Janie's father.

Joe Manchester.

CHAPTER THIRTY-NINE

"PUT your weapons down or I'm going to shoot!" Robertson pressed the gun into Joe's side.

Robertson's nostrils flared, his cheeks were red, and his eyes almost looked dilated.

Cassidy remained still, not wanting to make any sudden moves. Her gaze shifted to Joe.

He trembled next to Robertson.

He didn't match the pictures Cassidy had seen of him.

Yes, he was the same man. But, unlike in his photos, Joe's hair was now disheveled, stains wrecked his white shirt—including blood—and his eyes looked haggard.

What had that man been through over the past several days?

"I mean it! I'll shoot him!" Robertson said. "Don't test me."

Cassidy turned her head just slightly, enough so everyone could hear her. She'd taken lead on this—and the success or failure of the situation was on her shoulders.

"Everyone, stand down!" Cassidy called.

She had no doubt Robertson meant his words.

Around her, everyone lowered their weapons to the ground.

Robertson's gaze went to Governor Hollick. "You. You need to get over here."

Hollick visibly tensed beside her, and he raised his hands. "Richard . . . let's talk this out."

Politicians might be known for sweet-talking people. But Cassidy had a feeling that wouldn't work in this situation. Robertson was done with talking and now he only wanted Hollick to pay.

"This is no time for talking!" Robertson growled. "That opportunity has passed. You wouldn't even acknowledge what you did!"

Hollick raised his hands even higher. "I can explain . . ."

"I don't want to hear your excuses! It's time for you to pay the price." His voice rose in outrage and he took in ragged breaths.

This man was clearly unhinged.

Hollick trembled, his usual confidence beginning to disappear. "What do you want from me?"

Robertson's eyes narrowed. "Your life."

Cassidy's throat tightened when she heard the malice in the man's voice.

She was going to have to rely on all her police training—and God—to get out of this one.

"You need to come with me." Robertson's eyes fastened on Hollick. "Or the good doctor will die."

PETER STEPPED FORWARD, his entire body tense and ready for action.

He almost reminded Cassidy of a commando about to go rogue.

Her apprehension climbed higher.

That wouldn't help the situation here.

"He's not going anywhere with you," Peter growled, glowering at Robertson.

Cassidy's stomach clenched even more.

Robertson sneered. "I didn't ask for your permission."

"Let the governor go," Peter said. "This isn't going

to work out the way you think it is. I'm going to make sure of that."

Cassidy's eyes burned holes into Peter.

What was he even thinking right now? She tried to send him silent messages, but he either didn't get the hint or he didn't care. Both options were possible.

"Don't test me. I will shoot him." Robertson pushed the gun further into Joe until Joe let out a moan.

"Nobody needs to get hurt here." Cassidy kept her voice steady, not wanting to trigger the man. "Why don't you let Joe go and we can talk about things? We can talk about how the governor wronged you. About how if your funding hadn't been rejected, your wife might still be alive right now."

Robertson's gaze jerked toward Cassidy. "I've been watching you. You're a good cop."

"I try," Cassidy said. "I like to look out for the people around me. Just like you tried to look out for your wife."

Robertson's gaze went back to Hollick, his eyes still wide and deranged. "It's all his fault. He ruined my life. All for selfish gain. I'm sure he pocketed some of that money that he allotted for his brother's pharmaceutical company."

Hollick stepped back. "It wasn't like that. I promise you."

"Don't lie to me! That's all you ever do. You lie to people, you destroy innocent lives, and you get away with it. And I'm tired of people like you getting away with everything."

Hollick drew in a series of ragged breaths, exhaling in quick bursts. Sweat beaded on his forehead. "How can I prove to you that I didn't get a kickback from this?"

"It's too late for that. You've proven yourself to be a liar. And liars need to pay a price. That's why you need to come with me."

"You taking the governor away from here is a bad idea," Cassidy said. "It's only going to make the situation worse for everybody involved. Including you."

"It's the only way I can teach him a lesson. Now, come here, Hollick, before I pull this trigger."

"I don't know what you're thinking," Peter injected. "You're just going to end up in jail when we take you down for this. You need to put your gun down."

Again, Peter's tone only worked to get Robertson

more riled up. Cassidy could see the man's eyes harden every time Peter spoke.

"I want everyone out of here. Everyone but the governor. The governor and you." Robertson nodded at Cassidy.

"Me?" Cassidy tried to figure out his game plan, but it was useless.

"You're plucky. I like you. You stay. Everyone else goes except the governor."

"That's not happening," Peter said.

"Leave or he dies. You have until I count down from ten. Starting now. Ten. Nine. Eight . . ."

Cassidy glanced at the governor, then Peter. Based on Peter's gaze, he wasn't going to back down on this.

"Please. I have a wife. A daughter." Desperation stained Joe's tone.

"Three. Two . . ."

Joe let out another cry.

"Everyone, listen to the man," Hollick said. "Leave. This is my battle. And this innocent man shouldn't have to suffer. I want these grounds cleared now."

CHAPTER FORTY

"GOVERNOR, I CAN'T DO THAT." Peter stared at him, his shock evident. His gaze almost looked stupefied at Hollick's words.

"That's an order." The governor's voice hardened with conviction. "I want you to leave."

Peter's jaw flexed. "It's my job to protect you."

"I'm not willing to have these people die because of something I did. Now leave." Hollick's voice left no room for argument.

Cassidy nodded toward the men she'd brought with her. Reluctantly, they backed away from the scene.

She had no doubt they'd stay close, though.

But for now having everybody clear out was the

best thing they could do. She agreed with Hollick on that front.

Hollick turned to Cassidy. "You should leave too. This isn't about you."

"No!" Robertson's jaw clenched. "I said she needs to stay."

Cassidy nodded, trying to defuse the situation. "I'll stay if that's what you want."

But she had no idea what this guy was planning. Part of her didn't want to know.

With one more glance at them, Peter shook his head and began walking away.

Then it was just the four of them and a helicopter.

Cassidy held her breath, knowing that she couldn't let Robertson make this next move. It would give him too much control. She needed to take the reins of this situation.

"You got what you wanted." Cassidy was careful to keep her voice calm. "What is it that you need now?"

Robertson's dark hair was wet—probably with sweat. His motions were jerky. But it was his eyes that scared her the most—they were strangely passionate yet detached.

"You guys are coming with me," Robertson said.

"What's that going to prove?" Cassidy asked. "Can't we just talk here? There's no need to go and do your dirty deeds elsewhere."

"The world needs to know what a bad man he is." Robertson stared at Hollick.

Cassidy had to convince him this was a bad idea. "Just because he did something bad doesn't mean you need to ruin the rest of your life. There are other ways to get justice. Better ways than personal vengeance. Why not let Dr. Manchester go? He's innocent in all this."

"He wasn't part of my plan." Robertson's words took on a bitter drip. "But everything got messed up after Annabeth."

Cassidy's gaze went to Joe. It was clear the man was getting weaker and weaker.

Was there more to this? She assumed the man was dehydrated. That he'd been beaten.

But what if something else had happened to him?

Her gaze slid back to Robertson. "What was your plan?"

The first hint of a smirk pulled at Robertson's lips. "I'm glad you asked. I actually came up with a synthetic drug formula that mimics the symptoms of ALS. All Joe had to do was inject this cocktail into

Governor Hollick when he went in for his physical next week. He was already supposed to get a vaccination, so all Manchester here had to do was to manipulate the injection. It would have all been done."

A clearer picture formed in Cassidy's mind—a clearer but chilling picture. "What happened?"

Robertson's smirk disappeared, replaced with a heated stare, directed first at Cassidy and then the doctor. "Joe here, and his wife, decided to bend the rules. Things were going smoothly until a storm popped up. We had to pull our boat closer to land—and the closest land mass just happened to be Lantern Beach."

"You were keeping the family on a boat?" Cassidy remembered that drawing that Janie had made of the people on the boat and the child in the water. She held back a shiver as more details unfolded.

Robertson smirked again. "That's right. Taking them out on the water was the easiest way not to be found—not that anyone missed them. I had it all planned out. I made it look like they took a spontaneous trip to the Bahamas. I made sure to keep my ears open for any news indicating people were concerned about the family. But I covered my tracks well. No one suspected a thing."

"So what happened?" Cassidy continued.

She had to buy some time. Maybe she could talk some sense into this man. She had to at least try.

"Mom-and-Dad-of-the-Year decided it would be a good idea to put a life jacket on their daughter and throw her into the sea. They decided it was worth the risk and that Annabeth was safer there than she'd be in the boat."

"That's because you threatened to kill Joe's wife and daughter if he didn't do what you said, right?" The words left a sour taste in Cassidy's mouth.

Robertson sneered. "Leverage is very important in these matters. Yes, that is what I told him."

"We were close to the shore." Joe's voice cracked as he tilted forward, looking as if he could barely stand. "We had to try and save her. Looking at the water, I could tell how the currents were running. Sure, it was a risk. But it seemed like it was worth taking."

Cassidy's gaze met his. "And you put my name on a life jacket?"

Maybe this wasn't the time to ask that question, but Cassidy did anyway. She desperately wanted answers.

Joe perked up, hope and fear flashing in his eyes. "You found the life jacket? Annabeth . . . is she . . . ?"

"We have Annabeth," Cassidy assured him. "She's safe."

Joe nearly went limp in Robertson's arms—but not before flashing a grateful smile. "Thank you . . ."

Before he could ask any more questions, Cassidy asked again, "How did you know to use my name on the life jacket?"

"My family came here on vacation last summer," Joe continued, his voice raspy. "Someone told us about the EMP on the island and how you helped save this whole area from an imminent terrorist attack. It seemed like you were someone who could be trusted. If someone found Annabeth and was able to get her to you, we knew she'd be safe."

Cassidy's heart pounded as more things began to make sense. The desperation they must have felt to do what they did . . . she couldn't even imagine.

"Enough talking!" Robertson's nostrils flared. "We're wasting valuable time. Everybody in the helicopter. Now."

TY STARTED down the hall with Janie when Griff appeared from the stairway. Based on the way his friend's chest rose and fell, something had happened.

Hollick's escort hadn't gone as planned, had it?

Was Cassidy okay?

Griff lowered his voice. "We need you outside."

When Ty heard his friend's tone, his muscles tensed. "What's going on?"

Griff glanced at Janie before stepping closer. "Robertson is here. He hijacked the helicopter somehow, and he's taken the governor and Cassidy captive."

Ty's heart thudded in his chest.

He had to get to Cassidy.

Now.

But he glanced down at Janie. He couldn't leave the girl.

Tension rumbled in his chest.

"Janie can stay with Bethany and Ada. I can take her there now if you want me to." Griff's tone lightened as he glanced at the girl. "I think they're going to make some homemade playdough today. Does that sound fun?"

Janie said nothing—yet her eyes said everything. She was on board.

Ty knelt in front of Janie, feeling like this could be a pivotal moment. "I'll be back soon. I just need to check on something. When I get back, we'll go for a walk. Okay?"

Janie nodded.

Ty exchanged another glance with Griff before leaving Janie in his care. His steps quickened as he hurried outside.

The thought of Cassidy being held at gunpoint by a maniac like Richard Robertson made him feel sick. Though he trusted his wife's judgment and knew that her training was solid, nothing ever prepared someone to have their loved one directly in harm's way.

As soon as Ty got outside, he glanced around. Everyone had moved to the edges of the airfield. Without guns.

Four people stood by the helicopter—one of them being Cassidy.

Colton darted toward him, tension etched across his features.

"What's going on?" Ty rushed.

Colton nodded at the helicopter in the distance. "Robertson told everyone to leave except for Hollick and Cassidy. If we didn't, he threatened to shoot Dr. Manchester. Hollick and Cassidy both insisted we do as he said."

Ty's hands went to his hips. That didn't surprise

him. Cassidy always put others before herself. He wished she hadn't done that this time.

His heart panged at the thought of something happening to her.

But he couldn't focus on his emotions. He had to focus on the facts.

He glanced at Colton. "What's happened since then?"

"They all appear to be talking." Colton nodded toward them, his square jaw thumping between words. "Based on the way Robertson keeps looking at the helicopter, he wants everyone to get inside."

Ty chomped down, grinding his teeth at the thought. "That would be a bad idea. Who knows where he would take them?"

"Exactly. In the meantime, we're all waiting for a sign as to what to do next. Cassidy and the governor are calling the shots here."

Ty scanned the area around them—beyond law enforcement. "What about the other people this Robertson guy hired? Anyone have any idea where they went?"

Colton shook his head, his gaze darkening. "We've been monitoring the woods around the Blackout complex. We haven't seen them. But we're all on guard and at your disposal."

Ty's heart pounded against his ribs.

The last thing he wanted to do was stand back and wait.

But it looked like he had no choice. Cassidy could handle herself.

But there were still no guarantees in situations like this.

"She's going to get through this, Ty." Colton seemed to read his thoughts. "I know Cassidy. She's smart and tough."

Ty nodded, grateful for the reassurance.

He only wished it made him feel better.

CHAPTER FORTY-ONE

BASED on the unhinged way that Richard Robertson spoke and acted, it wouldn't surprise Cassidy if he planned to kill them all—including himself.

That was one more reason why she couldn't get in that helicopter with him.

No one would ever see her again.

Her gaze went to Robertson. She had to give everything she had left inside her—every last burst of energy—in order to reach him. It was her only chance right now.

Cassidy swallowed hard before asking, "Where are the people you hired?"

Robertson's gaze darkened. "Stop with all these

questions! I can see it was a mistake to keep you around after all. Maybe I should remedy that."

He pulled his gun away from Joe just long enough to point it at Cassidy. Based on the soulless look in his gaze, he wouldn't hesitate to pull the trigger.

Cassidy raised her hands, desperate to calm the man down.

Her heart thudded in her ears as she waited for his next move.

Finally, Robertson shoved the gun back into Joe's side. The man yelped.

Empathy churned inside her.

That man needed help—and soon.

Could Cassidy reason with someone with no heart?

That wasn't the case here, she reminded herself.

Robertson had loved his wife—all signs indicated that he'd loved her deeply.

Deeply enough to reach this point.

This guy wasn't soulless—he was just misled. His energies were misplaced. His grief had overtaken him, leading him to this point.

She needed to use that somehow.

Cassidy licked her lips, deciding to change tactics. "I just want some answers before I die.

Because that's what you're planning for all of us, isn't it? You're going to kill everyone here, aren't you? Including yourself."

Hollick sucked in a breath before casting a quick glance at her. She felt the fear emanating from him at her words. But this was no time to hold his hand and make him think everything would be fine.

"Why would you say that?" Robertson demanded as he leered at Cassidy.

Cassidy shrugged. "It's just the nature of this situation. I'm trying to put myself in your shoes, and that's the only plan of action I can think of that would give you any satisfaction. You've been lost since your wife died, haven't you?"

Robertson's chin trembled. "Allison was my whole world. All I wanted was to save her. I failed. Because of this man."

Robertson's face hardened again as he stared at Hollick, bitterness overtaking him.

Exactly what Cassidy didn't want to happen.

"It's hard losing the people we love," Cassidy continued. "It's *really* hard. But is this what Allison would have wanted?"

"Don't talk about my wife." Robertson's nostrils flared.

Cassidy kept her voice calm in order not to

trigger the man. "You hired that other couple, the Shacklefords. First, you hired them to pretend like they were Annabeth's parents."

"But you squashed that idea." Robertson scowled again.

"Why did you have them kill the couple staying in the home beside Governor Hollick? I'm still trying to make sense of that one."

Robertson's gaze narrowed even more. "They didn't have to die. But then they got nosy. They saw my guys over at the governor's place. All I wanted was to scope the place out, just in case. But those people saw my guys there and confronted them. The Shacklefords did what they had to do."

"I see. And you took these people's binoculars so no one would put it together that they might have seen something."

"Exactly! That's what I do. I check and double-check each detail." Robertson's gaze snapped back to the governor. "Enough talking. We all need to get into this helicopter. Now!"

That was a terrible idea.

Cassidy had to think of a way to detour from the helicopter without getting them all shot.

And she had to think of that way quickly.

Especially as Robertson turned his gun away

from Joe and toward Cassidy.

TY'S HEART lodged in his throat when he saw Robertson turn his gun toward Cassidy.

Ty reached for the weapon holstered at his waist.

But he knew he was too far away to shoot the man.

He needed to get closer.

Just as he took a step, a footstep sounded behind him.

Then a small voice yelled, "No!"

He jerked his head back.

Janie stood there.

Her eyes were fastened on the scene in the distance.

She'd spoken!

If only Ty could concentrate on that now.

Right now, he had to get the girl out of here.

Thankfully, from the far distance, she shouldn't be able to make out any details.

Ty prayed that was the case, at least.

Bethany bolted outside, a frantic look on her face.

"Go back!" Ty yelled before swooping Janie in his

arms. He sprinted back toward the building. "You aren't supposed to be out here."

Janie let out a cry in his arms.

"Everything's going to be okay," Ty murmured. "I need you to wait inside though, okay?"

He set her down in the entrance of the building.

"I'm so sorry," Bethany rushed, her hands going to Janie's shoulders. "One minute she was making a snowman out of play dough and the next—"

"It's okay." Ty knew he had no time to waste. "I have to get back outside. Whatever you do, keep Janie inside. Okay?"

Bethany nodded, apology in her eyes.

Ty would reassure her more later.

Right now, he leaned toward Janie one more time. "I need to go help outside. But I can't help if I think you're going to come out. So I need you to stay in here and play with Ada. Can you do that?"

She nodded.

Ty gave her a quick hug before jogging back outside.

As he did, he spotted Cassidy and the governor stepping toward the helicopter.

They really were going to leave together, weren't they?

Ty couldn't let that happen.

CHAPTER FORTY-TWO

"WAIT!" Cassidy yelled.

Robertson stopped and turned toward her.

"My friend is a reporter," she rushed. "Why don't you let me call her? She'll come here and do an interview with you. Then you can tell everybody what the governor has done."

Robertson continued to glower and bitterness dripped from his words. "I tried to go to reporters with my story. But the governor has them all in his pocket. No one listened to me. No one believed me. It's just one more reason I had to take these extreme measures."

"That must have been very frustrating for you," Cassidy said. "But my friend would listen. Wouldn't that be better than doing things this way? If you let me help you Hollick will have to live with his mistakes."

Robertson shook his head before sending a heated glance to the governor. "He'll probably just get away with it. That's what always happens with men like him."

"But maybe he wouldn't. Maybe you can be the change that you're looking to make."

Hollick's breaths became more shallow as he listened to the conversation. Anxiety emanated from him. Finally, he said, "I could do that. I'll do an interview. I'll tell people what I did."

Robertson's gaze swung toward him, skeptism lingering in the depths of his eyes. "You will?"

"I will." Sweat covered Hollick's face.

Robertson stared at him a moment before snapping from his gaze. He shook his head and chuckled, wagging his gun at Hollick like a teacher tsk-tsking a student. "There you go. You're still not owning up to anything, are you?"

"I am." Hollick's words sounded more high-pitched than usual. "I *will*. There's no way that my position with the state would survive something like that. You'll have the revenge that you want. I'll be done."

Robertson didn't say anything.

He was considering it, Cassidy realized.

Maybe she'd get through to him after all.

Robertson's eyes went back to her. "How quickly do you think your reporter friend could be here?"

Cassidy glanced at her watch. "I'm going to guess two hours. That is, if she's able to secure travel. She'll be coming down from the D.C. area."

Robertson's gaze narrowed. "How do I know you're not tricking me?"

"I can give you her name. You can research her yourself."

As he stared at her another moment, Cassidy waited.

He was going to say yes. She could feel it in her bones.

But she held her breath anyway.

Just as Robertson opened his mouth, a bullet blew through the air.

The shot barely missed him, lodging into the helicopter instead.

Cassidy's gaze darted toward the shooter.

Peter stood near the back of the helicopter, his gun raised and that rogue look still present in his eyes. He was trying to be the hero here.

The air whooshed from her lungs.

No . . . !

Cassidy had been so close.

Her gaze swung back to Robertson.

His gun was aimed at the governor, and he looked ready to act at any second.

TY GRIPPED HIS GUN.

He had no idea what was about to happen, but he knew it wasn't going to be good.

Peter had pulled the trigger.

And he'd done it right when it looked like Cassidy had been on the verge of taking control of the situation.

Ty had seen it in her posture, even in her expression.

But now all that was undone.

Ty's gaze fastened on the scene.

He couldn't let that man hurt Cassidy.

Around him, law enforcement and the Blackout team had drawn their weapons.

They all crept closer, trying to find cover in case the man pulled the trigger again.

Ty removed the safety on his own gun and put his finger on the trigger.

Then he watched.

The instant Robertson tried to shoot Cassidy, Ty was going to act.

Cassidy wasn't going down . . . not if he had anything to do with it.

CHAPTER FORTY-THREE

AS MORE GUNFIRE ERUPTED, Cassidy tackled the governor. They hit the concrete hard.

Hollick moaned beneath her as Cassidy's body shielded his from any danger.

Cassidy looked to the side, trying to catch a glimpse of what was going on.

Robertson still stood there by the copter. But he grimaced as if in pain and his free hand grasped his shoulder.

Someone had shot him . . .

He seemed to feel Cassidy's gaze on him and turned toward her.

His eyes narrowed.

Robertson might be shot, but he wasn't done—not until he drew his last breath.

Cassidy braced herself for pain. The man would pull the trigger. She saw it in his eyes.

She had nowhere to go. Nowhere to run. Nothing to use as protection.

In the distance, people scurried.

Cassidy swung her head to the sound, trying to get an idea of what was going on.

She looked over in time to see Colton tackle Peter.

The rest of the team had edged closer, moving in on Robertson.

But it might be too late.

Cassidy was the only thing separating Robertson from getting what he wanted: the governor dead.

Joe still stood beside Robertson, but the doctor looked on the verge of collapse.

Time seemed to slow as Cassidy braced herself for whatever was about to happen.

Her gaze met Robertson's.

"Don't do this." Cassidy's voice trembled.

He offered one last smirk as he raised his gun toward her.

Cassidy held her breath.

Her gaze went to the man's hand.

To his trigger finger.

It was twitching . . .

Just as he was about to pull the trigger, a gunshot exploded in the air.

Cassidy froze.

Where had the bullet come from? Where had it gone?

Had it hit her?

Was she in so much shock that she didn't realize it yet?

Then she saw the blood spreading across Robertson's chest.

He sank to the ground.

Wasting no time, Cassidy sprang to her feet. She kicked Robertson's gun away and watched as the man's eyes closed. He was beginning to fade.

He was no longer a threat to anyone here.

Cassidy's knees nearly went weak at the realization.

She reached for something to hold herself up, but there was nothing.

Until someone rushed to her and lifted her off her feet.

She looked up, and her heart burst with relief.

Ty.

He was okay.

And everything would be okay.

"Are you hurt?" Concern filled Ty's gaze, and his heart raced beneath her.

Cassidy shook her head before glancing down at the governor.

He was okay also—bruised. Humiliated. Possibly done ever holding office again.

But okay.

One of his security detail helped Hollick to his feet. Meanwhile, officers surrounded Robertson, and Colton rushed toward Dr. Manchester.

It looked like this was all over.

But the cleanup had just begun.

CASSIDY LOOKED BACK in time to see Dr. Manchester sink to the ground.

Had he been hit by a bullet?

Cassidy gently moved from Ty's arms to get a better look.

Colton knelt beside him, still assessing his injuries.

Manchester could barely keep his eyes open.

But his gaze found Cassidy and he muttered, "He . . . injected me."

Cassidy's eyes widened. "Who did? Robertson?"

Manchester tried to open his eyes again but didn't seem able. Instead, he licked his lips. "Yes."

Cassidy quickly pressed her eyes closed before leaning closer. "Do you know what he injected you with?"

"Don't . . . know." The doctor's voice was barely audible.

If she had questions for him, she had to ask now. The man was fading quickly.

"Where's your wife?" Cassidy's palms dug into the concrete as she bent toward him, silently begging him to hang on. Not just for her sake. But for Janie's.

"Don't . . . know."

Did that mean the bad guys still had her? Just how many people were involved here? Cassidy had no idea.

"Is there anything else that you can tell us?" Cassidy continued, hopeful for more answers.

Manchester's gaze fluttered to meet hers. "Find . . . Alexandria."

Cassidy nodded. "We won't give up. We'll look for her. I promise."

Just then, Manchester seemed to get a burst of strength. He grabbed Cassidy's hand, and his eyes opened as he muttered, "Take care of . . . Annabeth . . . please."

"Of course." Cassidy's voice cracked as emotion clogged her throat. "I won't let anything happen to her."

"Promise . . ."

Tears pressed her eyes. "I promise."

Then the doctor went limp.

No!

As a cry escaped from Cassidy, Ty pulled her away.

Just then, an ambulance pulled onto the scene.

At least this was finally over.

For now.

But Cassidy still had to tell Janie—Annabeth, Cassidy realized she should call her now—something about her parents.

How was she going to break the news without shattering the girl's heart? Her mother was missing. And her father . . .

What if he didn't make it?

She had no idea what she was going to say.

CHAPTER FORTY-FOUR

CASSIDY AND TY decided to wait until the next morning to talk to Annabeth.

The girl had been sleeping when they'd arrived back to get her after the fiasco on the airfield, and they'd decided to let her rest while she could.

They also wanted to see how Joe Manchester was doing at the hospital before they broke any news to her.

Apparently, Manchester was currently in a vegetative state. Doctors still weren't sure what kind of medication had been given to him, and Richard Robertson wasn't talking. Most likely, it was the same synthetic drug Robertson had originally wanted to give to Hollick.

Richard Robertson had also been treated for his

gunshot wound. Though he was being treated now, he'd be going to jail soon and facing some very stiff charges.

An investigation had been opened against Governor Hollick, but Cassidy anticipated the process would be lengthy. Most likely, it would be months before any conclusions—or charges—were filed.

Meanwhile, the story about the attempt on the governor's life had made national news, and Mac had taken the lead as the spokesperson for Lantern Beach. Governor Hollick had thanked the Lantern Beach Police Department and said that, without them, he would be dead right now.

Then he'd mentioned Cassidy's name.

Cassidy leaned back on the couch. Nausea rose in her every time she thought about it.

As soon as the story had broken, she'd started fielding calls from reporters.

The last thing she needed was for one of them to show up and start getting nosy.

But she'd have to face that obstacle when—and if—it came.

The good news was that Ty, Cassidy, Annabeth, and Kujo were going to move back into the cottage later today. The guys from Blackout were going to take turns keeping an eye on the place—at least until the Shacklefords were arrested.

With Robertson out of the picture, Annabeth should be safe.

But they couldn't take any chances.

Right now, she and Ty waited for Annabeth to wake up.

It was the first real opportunity Ty and Cassidy had to speak to each other alone. Cassidy had been too busy on the scene, talking to the FBI who'd been called in, and filing reports.

Ty had been a real trooper. He'd even put together a homemade breakfast casserole for them. It baked in the oven now, the scent of eggs and sausage floating through the air.

Ty took another sip of his coffee before asking, "Did you really know that reporter you mentioned to Robertson?"

Cassidy shook her head. "No, I didn't."

"What if Robertson had made you call her? What were you going to do?"

"I was going to wing it."

He shook his head and let out an airy chuckle. "You've got guts."

Cassidy wasn't so sure about that. She'd felt death. It had been close.

She was grateful to be here now.

"I was desperate," she finally admitted.

"Any updates on Peter?" Ty continued. "He took matters into his own hands and could have gotten everyone killed as a result."

Her stomach clenched at the mention of the man's name. "Last I heard, Hollick fired him. That man shouldn't be in security. I don't care what anyone says. He had something to prove, and that's never a good thing. Agendas cloud your judgment."

"I agree."

Before they could talk any more, Cassidy's phone rang.

It was the hospital.

She stood to answer and paced over into the kitchen area.

But the news wasn't what she'd hoped.

Joe's condition remained the same.

Ty frowned when she told him the news.

"How about Alexandria?" he asked.

"The search for her has been expanded outside this area since we don't believe she's being held here," Cassidy said. "But we still have no idea where Alexandria is. The Shacklefords could be holding her. The good news is that the FBI is now involved. Maybe we'll make more progress."

As she finished speaking, footsteps pattered down the hall.

Annabeth was awake.

Dread pooled in Cassidy's stomach.

Ty glanced at Cassidy, the strain obvious in his eyes. "Are you ready to talk to her?"

After a touch of hesitation, Cassidy nodded. She and Ty had already decided what they were going to tell her about what had happened. But Cassidy dreaded this conversation. Dreaded how it could only add more trauma to an already fragile girl.

She hadn't spoken still—only to yell, "No!"

Neither Ty or Cassidy had any idea if she'd seen her father or had any clue what was happening.

According to Ty, Dr. Manchester was standing behind Robertson when Annabeth came out.

If anything, it seemed like the girl had seen Robertson holding the gun to Cassidy instead.

But since she wasn't communicating, they couldn't be certain.

Ty offered his hand, and Cassidy took it. He pulled her toward him and kissed her forehead. Then Annabeth walked into the room.

Kujo walked over, tail wagging, to greet her.

Cassidy patted the space on the couch between her and Ty, motioning for Annabeth to come sit.

She did.

Then Ty started. "Listen, I know you're probably wondering what happened to your mom and dad. I want you to know that the bad guy who did this to your family won't be hurting anybody again."

Annabeth's eyes lit.

"Your dad is in the hospital right now, and doctors are trying to make him all better," Ty continued. "In the meantime, we have a lot of people out looking for your mom."

The girl's chin trembled.

Cassidy took her hand and squeezed it, wishing she could do more to take away the girl's pain.

"The good news is, until we find your mom and until your dad is out of the hospital, you're going to stay here with us." Ty's voice brightened. "Ms. Gail, the social worker, said that it was okay. The paperwork has already been filled out."

Cassidy held her breath, waiting for the girl's reaction.

The next instant, Annabeth threw her arms around Ty and buried herself in his chest. After his moment of surprise passed, Ty wrapped his arms around her too.

The sight of it warmed Cassidy's heart.

Maybe she and Ty wouldn't have any children of

their own. She didn't know. But there would always be children they could help. Children that might even feel like their own. Children who might come to think of Ty and Cassidy's house as their own.

She and Ty didn't know yet what they were going to do or how they were going to proceed. They would continue to pray about what to do.

Ty had been the one who'd pulled the trigger. Who'd stopped Robertson from shooting her.

He was—and always would be—her hero.

Cassidy glanced at Annabeth again and smiled. For now, Cassidy would concentrate on this little girl that had been entrusted to their care.

She was thankful this little game of hide-and-seek was finally over . . . for now.

~~~

If you enjoyed this book, please leave a review!

For updates on all future books, sign up for Christy's newsletter at: www.christybarritt.com.

Thank you so much for reading!
~~~

SHOCK AND AWE: COMING FEBRUARY 23!

COMPLETE BOOK LIST

Squeaky Clean Mysteries:

#1 Hazardous Duty

#2 Suspicious Minds

#2.5 It Came Upon a Midnight Crime (novella)

#3 Organized Grime

#4 Dirty Deeds

#5 The Scum of All Fears

#6 To Love, Honor and Perish

#7 Mucky Streak

#8 Foul Play

#9 Broom & Gloom

#10 Dust and Obey

#11 Thrill Squeaker

#11.5 Swept Away (novella)

#12 Cunning Attractions

#13 Cold Case: Clean Getaway

#14 Cold Case: Clean Sweep

#15 Cold Case: Clean Break

#16 Cleans to an End

While You Were Sweeping, A Riley Thomas Spinoff

The Sierra Files:

#1 Pounced

#2 Hunted

#3 Pranced

#4 Rattled

The Gabby St. Claire Diaries (a Tween Mystery series):

The Curtain Call Caper

The Disappearing Dog Dilemma

The Bungled Bike Burglaries

The Worst Detective Ever

#1 Ready to Fumble

#2 Reign of Error

#3 Safety in Blunders

#4 Join the Flub

#5 Blooper Freak

#6 Flaw Abiding Citizen

#7 Gaffe Out Loud

#8 Joke and Dagger

#9 Wreck the Halls

#10 Glitch and Famous (coming soon)

Raven Remington

Relentless 1

Relentless 2 (coming soon)

Holly Anna Paladin Mysteries:

#1 Random Acts of Murder

#2 Random Acts of Deceit

#2.5 Random Acts of Scrooge

#3 Random Acts of Malice

#4 Random Acts of Greed

#5 Random Acts of Fraud

#6 Random Acts of Outrage

#7 Random Acts of Iniquity

Lantern Beach Mysteries

#1 Hidden Currents

#2 Flood Watch

#3 Storm Surge

#4 Dangerous Waters

#5 Perilous Riptide

#6 Deadly Undertow

Lantern Beach Romantic Suspense

Tides of Deception

Shadow of Intrigue

Storm of Doubt

Winds of Danger

Rains of Remorse

Torrents of Fear

Lantern Beach P.D.

On the Lookout

Attempt to Locate

First Degree Murder

Dead on Arrival

Plan of Action

Lantern Beach Escape

Afterglow (a novelette)

Lantern Beach Blackout

Dark Water

Safe Harbor

Ripple Effect

Rising Tide

Lantern Beach Guardians

Hide and Seek

Shock and Awe

Safe and Sound

Crime á la Mode

Deadman's Float

Milkshake Up

Bomb Pop Threat

Banana Split Personalities

The Sidekick's Survival Guide

The Art of Eavesdropping

The Perks of Meddling

The Exercise of Interfering

The Practice of Prying

The Skill of Snooping

The Craft of Being Covert

Saltwater Cowboys

Saltwater Cowboy

Breakwater Protector

Cape Corral Keeper

Seagrass Secrets

Driftwood Danger

Carolina Moon Series

Home Before Dark

Gone By Dark

Wait Until Dark

Light the Dark

Taken By Dark

Suburban Sleuth Mysteries:

Death of the Couch Potato's Wife

Fog Lake Suspense:

Edge of Peril

Margin of Error

Brink of Danger

Line of Duty

Cape Thomas Series:

Dubiosity

Disillusioned

Distorted

Standalone Romantic Mystery:

The Good Girl

Suspense:

Imperfect

The Wrecking

Sweet Christmas Novella:

Home to Chestnut Grove

Standalone Romantic-Suspense:

Keeping Guard

The Last Target

Race Against Time

Ricochet

Key Witness

Lifeline

High-Stakes Holiday Reunion

Desperate Measures

Hidden Agenda

Mountain Hideaway

Dark Harbor

Shadow of Suspicion

The Baby Assignment

The Cradle Conspiracy

Trained to Defend

Mountain Survival

Nonfiction:

Characters in the Kitchen

Changed: True Stories of Finding God through Christian Music (out of print)

The Novel in Me: The Beginner's Guide to Writing and Publishing a Novel (out of print)

ABOUT THE AUTHOR

USA Today has called Christy Barritt's books “scary, funny, passionate, and quirky.”

Christy writes both mystery and romantic suspense novels that are clean with underlying messages of faith. Her books have won the Daphne du Maurier Award for Excellence in Suspense and Mystery, have been twice nominated for the Romantic Times Reviewers’ Choice Award, and have finaled for both a Carol Award and Foreword Magazine’s Book of the Year.

She is married to her Prince Charming, a man who thinks she’s hilarious—but only when she's not trying to be. Christy is a self-proclaimed klutz, an avid music lover who’s known for spontaneously bursting into song, and a road trip aficionado.

When she's not working or spending time with her family, she enjoys singing, playing the guitar, and exploring small, unsuspecting towns where people have no idea how accident-prone she is.

Find Christy online at:

www.christybarritt.com

www.facebook.com/christybarritt

www.twitter.com/cbarritt

Sign up for Christy's newsletter to get information on all of her latest releases here: **www.christybarritt.com/newsletter-sign-up/**

If you enjoyed this book, please consider leaving a review.

Made in the USA
Monee, IL
07 February 2021

59869622R00187